# BEAUTY
## FROM ASHES

Pamela Hart

ISBN 978-1-0980-9645-8 (paperback)
ISBN 978-1-0980-9647-2 (hardcover)
ISBN 978-1-0980-9646-5 (digital)

Christian Faith Publishing
832 Park Avenue
Meadville, PA 16335
www.christianfaithpublishing.com

All scripture references taken from the NIV, 2011 edition.

Printed in the United States of America

In memory of those who lost their lives in the 2011 Tōhoku earthquake and tsunami. You are not forgotten.

Place me like a seal over your heart,
like a seal on your arm;
for love is as strong as death,
its jealousy unyielding as the grave.
It burns like blazing fire,
like a mighty flame.
Many waters cannot quench love;
rivers cannot sweep it away.
If one were to give
all the wealth of one's house for love,
it would be utterly scorned.

—Song of Songs 8:6–7

# CHAPTER 1

"Don't hold back this time!"

"I can't make any promises!" Arnion gripped the flexi handles of his fuga and extended his arms forward, locking them into place with a smooth click.

Rhys grinned and pushed a button at his left temple, extending a yellow light shield across the upper portion of his face. "The usual rules. First one through the canyon and back without losing any petals wins."

Arnion nodded, patting the pocket on his chest where the five-petaled Chiksa blossom was nestled. Reaching down, he scooped up a handful of sand from the canyon ledge and let it slip through his fingers. It swirled gently in front of them, carried by the light breeze. "Wind looks good."

He spared a quick glance over the rim of the canyon where they hovered. Jagged rocks rose like spines from the walls and floor below. Their violent pink was a stark contrast against the brilliant blue sky. *What a view,* he mused, savoring it for a moment.

Hearing Rhys clear his throat beside him, Arnion turned back to his friend. His pale-blue light shield shimmered into place with a slight buzz. "You ready?" he quipped.

"Always" came the eager reply.

Arnion set the holographic timer on his fuga to three breaths.

"Three, two," the computer chimed, numbers swiping clockwise through the air in front of them, "one."

Both young men simultaneously dug their left foot into the ignition pad and leapt down into the canyon. The fuga left a crackling stream of blue electricity in their wake, moving too fast for the naked eye to follow. The only trace of the two Eirenians and their hovercraft was a slight waft of electrostatic discharge.

Arnion laughed as the wind whipped through his hair and caused the webbing on his white fibro jacket to ripple over his skin. He could feel the sun's warmth like a caress on his back. The fibro jacket automatically adjusted its internal temperature in response to the user's environmental and physical exertion, but with the cool breeze rising from the river below, it was hardly necessary.

Feeling the fuga hum with power beneath him, Arnion closed his eyes. Flying came so naturally to him. It was like breathing. He could feel the pull of the wind as they hurtled through the canyon. His instincts guided his hands in the minor adjustments needed to avoid crashing into the teeth-like projections crusting the walls. The rush of it all made him laugh with joy. Sparking down his fingers, the energy from his spirit seeped into the fuga. The engine roared with the fresh influx of power, and the hovercraft shot forward in a burst of speed.

Still chuckling, Arnion opened his eyes. He was almost at the turnaround point, but Rhys had fallen behind. His childhood friend teased him about holding back, but it was true. Arnion had never liked coming in first. Despite their earlier banter, the prince reached deep into his spirit and partially covered its fiercely burning light. The fuga whined pitifully and slowed its pace.

When Rhys realized that he was once more gaining on his friend, he shook his head with a sigh. *Sometimes Arnion is too kind for his own good. Well,* he grinned to himself, *I'll give His Majesty a flight to remember today.* Reaching down into a joyful childhood memory, Rhys fanned his spirit into a flame. His fuga radiated with newfound energy. The thrusters irised open with a boom, and the hovercraft rocketed forward. Now, he and the prince were neck and neck.

They were approaching the Eye of the Needle, the narrowest part of their route through the canyon. Even with a single fuga, it took a skillful rider to avoid the jagged pink rocks jutting out along the ledge. Rhys expected Arnion to suddenly burst ahead and clear the Needle before him. However, as the walls continued to narrow, his friend did not budge. Out of the corner of his eye, Rhys noticed the prince's head was tilted at a strange angle. Arnion had turned his fuga sideways and was weaving in between the rocks of the canyon wall.

Rhys laughed out loud in wonder. A quick glance over at his friend revealed that the prince's shoulders were shaking with laughter too. Even as they passed through the Needle and on toward the end of their route, Arnion continued to fly sideways. Rhys reached up to wipe a tear of laugher out of his eye. That's when he caught sight of something tiny and white fluttering through the air.

*Arnion's Chiksa! It must have slipped out during his practical joke,* Rhys thought frantically. *Arnion, you wouldn't!*

Exhaling sharply, Rhys watched as his friend scaled his fuga further up the canyon wall, arcing it until he was completely upside down. And then, Arnion let go.

Rhys would have screamed, but he was moving so fast that the wind tore the air from his throat as quickly as it left his lungs. He wrenched the flexi handles around and sped back toward where he had seen his friend fall.

*Arnion!*

For one breath, Rhys could see him free-falling through the air. The next moment, the prince's fuga came screaming back around, completing its sweep along the opposite canyon wall and landing neatly beneath its rider.

Maneuvering his fuga alongside Arnion's, Rhys set the machine to hover. "Are you out of your mind?" he shouted, taking hold of the prince's shoulders and shaking him fiercely. "What were you thinking?"

Arnion smiled and held out his right hand, cupped in a loose fist. As he opened it slowly, Rhys saw the white blossom resting undamaged in his palm.

"You risked your life for a child's game! Arnion, what were you thinking? How could I ever face your father, let alone the entire kingdom, if you were hurt?" With a shaking hand, he wiped the sweat from his brow. "It's a miracle your fuga didn't short out the minute you lost contact."

9

"I'm sorry, Rhys." Arnion looked down. The triumphant smile on his face melted away as he realized the depth of his friend's concern. "I've been meaning to show you I've figured out a way to steer the fuga even without direct contact. It's a little stunt I've been working on. I was perfectly safe. I'm sorry." The prince held out his hands, palm up in a gesture of repentance, and peeked up at his friend through his visor.

Arnion looked so utterly remorseful. Rhys let out a sigh of defeat. "How can anyone stay angry with you?" he relented, scratching the back of his neck. "Just give me a little more of a heads-up next time, all right?"

Rhys held out his hand, and Arnion took it, gripping tightly for a moment before letting go.

"How did you find time to practice something like that without me noticing?" Rhys asked. "You attend so many meetings and committees. It's amazing you can keep track of it all." At his friend's wry grin, Rhys persisted. "Do you still find time for those morning walks with your father?"

A genuine smile now kindled on Arnion's lips. "Every day."

At that moment, a gentle breeze blew through the canyon, ruffling their hair. It carried with it the stench of burning flesh and sulfur.

"Ugh!" Rhys pinched his nose closed in disgust. "I didn't realize you could smell Gehenna all the way from here!"

Arnion frowned. "You couldn't in the past. It's spreading." He reached down to adjust the fuga's control dials, releasing it from hover mode. The vehicle hummed as it returned to full power. "Let's head back. Father and his advisors will begin their meeting soon. There's talk of sending another ambassador in."

"Whoever it is will need a spirit of iron." Rhys toggled his controls, powering up his fuga as well. "The last few we've sent in have come back beaten or tortured. Nothing seems to get through to those people." He glanced over at Arnion, whose gaze was fixed on a smudge of dark smoke rising in the distance.

The prince tightened his grip on his flexi handles. "Let's go."

Without another word, he kicked the ignition pad and turned back toward the palace. Rhys followed at a respectful distance. Clearly, Arnion was no longer in the mood for games.

"The situation in Gehenna is getting out of hand!" Advisor Arsk banged on the meeting table with finality, the sound echoing up into the vaulted ceiling.

Seated next to him, Advisor Ayam flinched. Her normally buoyant personality always wilted a bit during talks about Gehenna. Since her appointment to the counsel table, wrinkles had begun to form at the outer edges of her eyes. Her shining auburn hair now accented with whorls of silver still looked stunning against the emerald green collar that fanned elegantly from her neck.

She twirled a silver stylus in her left hand, causing the light to flash off her beringed fingers. Clearing her throat, she conceded, "Our spies have reported numerous indications that Lucien will attack the palace."

"Nonsense," Advisor Genoas interrupted. "Even if Lucien threw a million bodies at us, he could never hope to overcome our defenses."

Ayam continued, brows knit together, "How many more lives must be sacrificed before his madness is stopped? We cannot, in good conscience, allow things to continue like this indefinitely." She turned questioning eyes toward the center of the room.

The royal throne was a masterpiece of Eirenian architectural ingenuity. King Elyon's chair had been carved out of a single emerald so pure that it was nearly translucent. A brilliant halo of rainbows refracted outward from its surface, painting the room in glimmering circles of light. Elegant golden columns spiraled upward from the floor, so slender and delicate. It seemed impossible that they could support the weight of the vaulted ceiling above. Thousands of refractor prisms had been painstakingly embedded between the ribbing of the roof, casting a perfect reflection of the sky. Indeed, many first-time visitors believed they had somehow wandered outside, so flawless was the illusion.

Even in silence, the king's presence was a powerful force, drawing others to him with a magnetism that could not be explained by his position alone. His chin rested in the palm of his hand, elbow propped up on the armrest of his chair. A finger tapped against his bottom lip. Astute eyes followed each speaker carefully.

At his right sat his only son, Prince Arnion. The young man watched his father closely. Amber eyes scanned the king's beloved, craggy face, trying to discern the thoughts hidden beneath. The prince's usually bright expression was cloudy, mouth pulled into a grim line.

Before the throne, the advisors continued their discussion, gestures becoming wilder, their voices raised and sharp. Genoas stood abruptly, hand slicing through the air like a knife.

"We should just wipe them out entirely, eliminate Lucien and his followers once and for all."

His outburst met with a few startled looks. As the youngest and most recently inducted member, he was still acclimating to his new role.

The king's brows knit together, and he held up his hand, palm out. Instantly, an expectant hush fell over those assembled. Every eye turned toward Elyon. His expression was solemn.

"I do not wish to harm those who have been lured in by Lucien's schemes. We must do everything in our power to secure their release."

His tone left no room for argument, and Genoas had the grace to look down, embarrassed.

Elyon continued, lowering his hand, "I know we have spent many years trying to expose Lucien's treachery and lies with little success. Even so, I have compassion on these people. Although they have chosen to separate themselves from us, their suffering breaks my heart."

The king's gaze sought out each of his advisors, one by one. "Is there anyone left who is willing to go? Anyone who still sees a hope in redeeming them?"

"I will go, Father." Arnion rose and brought his right fist up to rest above his heart and thumped it once against the jeweled armor of his breastplate. "Perhaps they will listen to me, your son."

"Out of the question!" Advisor Arsk exclaimed, cheeks turning an alarming shade of fuchsia. His pale hands fluttered above the folds of his amethyst robes. "You are His Majesty's sole heir, the future ruler of Eiren. You cannot put your life at risk in this manner."

Advisor Maulki held out a thick hand, calloused from heavy farmwork. "Maybe they would listen to him. We've sent everyone else even remotely suitable."

The advisor's resonant voice only helped to remind his audience of the calm strength coiled within him. Maulki was not given to recklessness or extravagance. Even his formal ocher tunic was embellished only by a thick braid of red and white cord that twined around his collar.

"Arnion's spirit ability *is* unprecedented," Advisor Ayam chimed in. "It could protect him from many of Gehenna's threats."

The delicate golden bells woven around the cuffs of her emerald gown tinkled with her movement. Her extravagant wardrobe always contrasted sharply against Maulki's simplicity. Despite their differences in taste however, the two had become fast friends over the years.

Again, arguing broke out around the room as the king's advisors tried to outshout each other, airing protests, suggestions, and horrified indignation. Suddenly, Elyon rose and turned to face his only child. Advisor Ark's jaw popped open in shock. A vein twitched in Genoas's throat. Standing eye to eye with his son, Elyon shared an entire conversation with one look.

"Have you truly considered the cost, my son?"

"Yes, Father. I have compassion on these people. They were once the same as any of us in this room. I believe that there is still hope to free them from Lucien's treachery."

"And what if you should fail?" It was Advisor Arsk again.

Arnion broke from his father's gaze to meet the other man's pointed stare. "In your darkest hour, a light will shine forth and lead you unto victory," he quoted the ancient Eirenian prophecy.

The advisor dropped his gaze to the floor and let out a long sigh.

The prophecy had been uttered hundreds of years ago, shortly after the time of the Fall. Everyone had assumed that it would spell a quick and utter destruction for the Deceiver, and yet he was still roaming the planet Elorah, free to sow chaos and sorrow wherever he went.

Elyon reached out and took hold of Arnion's left shoulder. He drew his son to himself and held him in a tight embrace. Tears pricked at the corners of his eyes, and he took a shuddering breath before letting go. Placing his hands firmly on Arnion's shoulders, he looked deeply into the face of his child, whose eyes sparkled with hope.

"Go, my son. You have my blessing," the king declared in a gravelly voice as a smile broke a familiar path through the hard lines of his face.

Arnion bowed deeply to his father and rose. The grin that had been tugging at the corners of his mouth finally burst forth as he met the king's eyes.

"Thank you, Father."

The purple cape latched at his shoulders whirled as he turned and strode boldly toward the inlaid doors at the back of the grand hall. He did not look back.

Rhys met him in the corridor.

"So you will be the next ambassador, Arnion?"

"Yes." Arnion grinned and ran a hand through his dark wavy hair. "Will you help me get ready?"

"Do you even need to ask?" Rhys quipped, holding up a tattered bundle of linen garments and a coarse woven belt. "They don't keep me cooped up in the ambassadorial sector just for my good looks, you know? I've got a knack for helping people blend into Gehenna. Would I really abandon my post, not to mention my best friend, now that his hour has come?"

Arnion knocked Rhys on the shoulder lightly with his fist.

Looking down at the floor, he said quietly, "I want to be just like them, Rhys. Nothing to make me stand out or draw attention to myself. Make me an eyesore if you have to." Curling his hand into a tight fist at his side, his voice became fierce. "I don't want to manipulate anyone with my appearance. I won't play games with them like Lucien. The only thing that should influence them is the truth." When he looked up, his golden eyes appeared almost aflame.

Rhys nodded at his friend's earnest expression. "You have so much of your father in you, Arnion," he said proudly. "Come, let's get you ready. I've got a lot of work to do if I'm to make someone as handsome as you look like a citizen of Gehenna."

# CHAPTER 2

Acadia gasped and bolted upright. She had been torn from her sleep by a shrill wail that pierced the darkness. Now, somewhere off in the distance, a voice was weeping uncontrollably. She shivered and wrapped her arms protectively in front of her chest. On her back, the fading scars from the guards' whips shone as white ridges in the moonlight. She slid her dirty, scabbed hands off her shoulders and down her arms, thankful that she no longer had blisters bubbling out beneath her palms. Acadia fought the urge to scratch at the rash spreading from her knuckles down her fingers and along her eyelids. Smoke rash they called it, caused by the firepits that constantly burned the refuse and human remains that were always threatening to engulf the city.

"You'll get used to the smell," they said.

She hadn't believed them, but she did.

Next to her, a bundle of rags squirmed, and the smudged face of one of her cellmates peaked out. "Can't sleep again?" the girl wheezed.

Acadia shook her head wryly.

"You'll get used to the crying," her cellmate murmured, rolling over and burrowing deeper into the filthy pile of rags that served as their bedding.

Acadia hung her head. Her once glossy black hair was now shorn to her scalp. *He told me he would make me beautiful,* she thought, digging her cracked fingernails into her arms, *but now, I am utterly repulsive.* Hot tears burned at the corner of her eyes, and she clenched her teeth to stifle the sobs of despair that tried to tear their way through her chest. *I am going to die here,* she felt in the pit of her heart. She could already hear them saying, "You'll get used to it."

A rattling sound creeping up the hall caused her to flinch instinctively. The guards were dragging their bludgeon sticks across the cage bars as they walked. Their guttural shouts reverberated off the rusting iron walls.

"Every one of you worthless maggots on your feet! Lucien has called a meeting. He wants to talk with you."

One guard was sneering into her cell, revealing crooked yellow teeth. Another's laughter devolved into a hacking cough, and he spit a wad of oozing mucus on the floor. Iron doors screeched open, and the prisoners shuffled out in a single ragged line.

"You lazy worm! On your feet now!"

One of the guards was bellowing into a cell on her right. Out of the corner of her eye, Acadia could see him yank the prisoner's arm. There was a popping sound, and suddenly, the prisoner's arm hung at a strange angle. The man was soaked in perspiration. His eyes rolled into the back of his head as the guard shook him.

"This one's done in. Take 'im to the pit."

Another guard cursed and kicked at the man before clamping his two scrawny wrists together and dragging him away.

Acadia and the other prisoners were herded into the courtyard. Pouring in from all sides were the people from the other containment areas. Their thousands of scuffing feet had kicked up a layer of soot and dust that stuck in their eyes and noses, coating everyone with a grimy film. In the center was an ominous black stage, normally reserved for the weekly spectacle.

*Didn't we just have one a few days ago?*

Acadia tried not to let the throng carry her too close to the stage. Lucien's latest victim had nearly crawled off the end of it, and the closer onlookers had been drenched in arterial spray. Restless murmurs flowed over the people. It seems Acadia wasn't the only one wondering if it was too early for another spectacle.

A strangled wave of silence spread out from the center as a lone figure ascended the stage. Lucien held his arms out wide and smiled at the crowd. Spotlights caused the metallic rings on his hands to send flashes of light twinkling over the audience. His velvety deep voice washed over them.

"My beloved people, I called you here today to discuss a startling rumor." Lucien contorted his ivory face into a pout. "It has reached my ears that Elyon, that simpering fool, may be sending another ambassador into our midst. I know that some of you have taken to calling me 'the Heartless King.' Quite unfairly, I might add." He held a martyred hand up to his forehead and closed his glittering jade eyes for a moment. Opening them again, he let out an exaggerated sigh.

"Have you forgotten that it was you who willingly bound yourselves to me? I came in good faith, offering gifts of wealth and power. Things which you would never have tasted under that incompetent bleeding heart, Elyon. Remember how quickly you ran to me? How you clung to me and begged me to bestow my gifts upon you? But then, when it came time to pay, you were not willing, my pets. So what else could I do but bring you here, to my home, until you've worked off your debt?"

Lucien stopped his pacing and held out a hand to the people gathered around him. "How can I make you see that I am not your enemy? Perhaps a show of my unending benevolence toward you. Thirty pieces of drakka for the man who brings me Elyon's ambassador!"

The volume and tone of his voice began to grow with every word, reaching a shrieking crescendo of sound that ricocheted off the walls.

"And double portions of rations for all so that you may be alert in routing him out! Listen for his lies! Watch for his foolish bleeding heart just like his master's! Bring him to me, your true king, and I will make him pay for your suffering!"

Acadia watched from the multitude as those around her began nodding and clapping. From the edges of the courtyard, the guards began stamping their feet and shouting raucously, "All hail King Lucien." Her eyes widened as the crowd began screaming in response.

"Lucien! Lucien!"

Discordant voices echoed through the courtyard growing louder and louder.

*This is bordering on hysteria.* Acadia looked down, biting her lip. *How can they keep falling for this?*

The cheers drilled into her skull from all sides. She felt nauseous. There was Lucien, parading around the stage, whipping the people into more and more of a frenzy. He was eating it up, tossing his golden head back as he laughed. With his stunning green eyes and chiseled features, he was terrifyingly beautiful.

After a moment more, Lucien seemed to grow bored with the attention.

"ENOUGH!" A single wave of his hand and the cry of the mob was strangled. "Now, my pets, go to your labor. Let no one repay my generosity with laziness. I expect you all to meet your quota. Remember our next weekly spectacle is just two days away."

Teeth flashing, he raised his right fist out toward the quarry, and the guards began jabbing those nearest to them with their bludgeon sticks, prodding them to the exits.

"All right, you miserable curs, back to work!"

The shouts of the guards were accompanied by purposeful blows on the prisoners not moving fast enough for their liking.

Acadia was letting herself be carried along when a hand clamped onto her left arm and yanked her to the side. A guard with pulsating red boils leered down at her.

"Thiz one'z not too bad, iz she Marco?"

She could feel his fetid breath like a moist wind across her face.

"Not bad at all, Tirion." Another guard rose from between the shadows at the edge of the courtyard, picking his nails with a small dagger. "She must still be new. See how 'er eyes don't have that dead look yet."

"We'll have to help her get uzed to the place." Tirion licked his lips and rubbed his hands together.

Acadia flinched and closed her eyes as she felt someone take hold of her hand.

"Don't be afraid," a voice whispered in her ear.

She squinted her right eye open slightly. A young man was standing next to her, holding her hand lightly in his. Smoke rash had spread all along the left side of his face, causing one eye to swell nearly shut. His skin was dry and scabby, even to her calloused hand. And when he spoke, she saw how his cracked lips bled.

"Let us pass." The young man had a clear voice.

The guards stumbled to the side, bewildered. The young man, still gripping her hand, gently but firmly pulled her past them. She realized as they walked that the man had an uneven stride, with a strong limp in his right leg. They continued along the footpath to the quarry until Acadia suddenly realized that they were still holding hands and snatched hers away.

"What were you thinking back there? They could've just as easily killed us both!" She avoided his eyes and settled for glaring at his dusty sandals instead.

"I'm not a prisoner. They have no authority over me." He turned his head right and left, gazing at everything around them as they walked.

"If you're not a prisoner, why are you here?" She crossed her arms in front of her chest.

"To rescue you."

She laughed in his face. "Did all Lucien's talk of ambassadors go to your head? Only a fool would come to Gehenna of their own free will. As far as I'm concerned, any citizen of Eiren that steps foot in these camps is already dead." She drew a finger across her throat as she spoke, revealing a streak of pale skin through the grime on her neck.

"Besides, it's said that all Elyon's people possess a beauty unmatched in Elorah. Do you really expect me to believe a scabby cripple like you just waltzed down from the royal courts?"

Acadia wanted to recoil at callousness of her own words.

*That was harsh, but this man was obviously crazy, wasn't he?*

Crazy people made her nervous. Crazy people got themselves and others around them killed.

The person in question met her eyes with a serious look. He didn't seem angry or ruffled by her comments, but he was looking at her intensely as if he could read the fear that raged within her and see her heart hammering through her chest. That encounter with the guards shook her up more than she wanted to admit. And yet, she felt more undone by the calm, searching gaze of the young man before her. It was unnerving.

"Stay away from me," Acadia muttered. Steeling herself against the traitorous shaking that had begun in her hands, she turned on her heel and stormed off.

# CHAPTER 3

"Wait!" Arnion called after her. The girl stomped away without looking back. He watched her thoughtfully until she turned around a curve of the quarry and abruptly vanished from his sight. It wasn't surprising she didn't trust him. The people here were ready to turn on each other for a scrap of bread. When he had seen those two guards heading toward her, he could read all the cruel thoughts flashing through their minds. Even if it revealed his identity earlier than he had planned, Arnion knew he had to intervene. It seemed that luck was on his side, however. No one seemed to notice or care about his actions. Arnion shook his head. At least his disguise seemed to be working.

*That girl,* he thought, *what had happened to her? How did a young woman like her end up in a place like Gehenna?* He couldn't imagine what kind of lies Lucien had woven to ensnare her heart and mind.

Arnion thought back to the day he had slipped behind Gehenna's borders.

*Has it already been thirty-two days? Or was today number thirty-three?* Arnion chuckled to himself. *Rhys was right.*

While his friend had been making the necessary preparations for the ambassadorial trip, he insisted over and over that the prince at least embed a fingerprint-sensitive data crystal in his forearm. The young royal could still remember the conversation vividly.

"Arnion, please, you're killing me! At least take the data crystal!" Rhys had pleaded. "It's the bare minimum for any agent on assignment, even within Eiren! Even your father wouldn't object to that."

At the stubborn look in the prince's eyes, Rhys had thrown up his hands in exasperation.

"How are you even going to tell how long you've been over there? You know Lucien deliberately represses information! It's his modus operandi to keep things confused and hazy. The less people realize their lives are bleeding away, the less likely they are to revolt."

Arnion shook his head. "I already told you I'm not going to take any of our tech with me. Those people don't need technology! They need compassion, human interaction, and most importantly, to be freed. There'll be plenty of time to introduce them to all the wonderful devices of Eiren *after* they've been released."

Rhys made one last attempt. "I can digitally code it to only be visible to your optic spectrum! No one else would even know it was there! It would only take me a moment." He gestured hopefully toward his cluttered workbench and waggled his eyebrows at Arnion.

"No," the prince had said firmly but with kindness in his eyes.

Rhys sighed and looked up to the sky. Ultimately, Arnion had the final word.

It was a testament to their strong friendship that he would argue with an ambassador as much as he had. Agents of Eiren were often selected because of their highly intuitive nature. They had an innate sense of what they would need to fulfill their mission, and Arnion was a member of the royal family at that. Still, the prince could tell that his friend wanted to argue further, but all Rhys said out loud was, "As you wish, Your Highness."

Shaking himself out of his reverie, Arnion couldn't help but touch the inner part of his forearm where the data crystal would have laid, a nearly imperceptible bump under his skin. An interactive display of calendar dates ranging five hundred years into both the past and the future would have just been the beginning of its features. It could send alerts back to Eiren, activate a remote tracking beacon, and scan forty-seven wavelengths beyond the visible spectrum. It included a nanoscopic audiovisual recording system, mineral and sustenance locator, a discreet poison sensor, and even an enemy surveillance detector.

*A truly useful survival device,* Arnion mused, but he didn't regret leaving it behind. *It wouldn't have been able to do anything about the smell here in any case.*

The stench when he had first entered Gehenna was overpowering. As Arnion had climbed the rock wall separating his kingdom from Lucien's, the smoke and malodorous air wafting over him were like a physical extension of the border, trying to push him away. He could feel the toxins of the smoke seeping into his skin, exaggerating the itchiness of the rash Rhys had recently induced on his face. He resisted the urge to scratch at his recently shorn head.

Then he had seen the people. Arnion had fallen to his knees and wept. Pale scarecrows with shadowy eyes, the people dragged themselves along. Some had bodies so gaunt you could count every vertebra along their spine, others with wrinkled, scabby skin hanging off them in folds, but all covered with the festering rash Gehenna was famous for. Their shaved heads were uncovered in the scorching heat, many with patches of dry skin peeling off their scalps.

A smiling guard viciously kicked out at a limping older man. As the man fell, the others continued to trudge over him, seemingly oblivious to his agonized screams as he was trampled to death.

Arnion watched as the people jostled each other along their way to the quarry each day. More than one life was snuffed out along that brutal march. It was as if they didn't even see each other as human anymore, only slabs of meat in their way. As the crowd dwindled off to their work zones, vaguely humanoid creatures with splotched skin scrabbled out from the rocks and began tearing at the corpses. They snarled at Arnion as he walked past, flicking out forked tongues.

*Kraggies*, he thought to himself. *These bottom-feeding scavengers must be well-fed in Gehenna.*

The oppression here was much worse than he ever could have imagined. The people looked out at him with hollow eyes. He wondered if they could even see anymore or if their bodies were shambling along through pure muscle memory.

Arnion sighed, his mind turning back to the present. Assimilating into their midst, if you could call it that, had been too easy. No one ever questioned him, talked to him, looked at him, or even acknowledged his existence. They seemed beyond all hope of freedom.

*Lucien has these people right where he wants them. It's no wonder so many of Eiren's ambassadors had failed. How am I ever going to get through to these people*, he wondered.

As the dusty wind pulled at his tunic, Arnion was drawn into a memory. He was a young boy with his father at the edge of the sea. The salty wind was pulling at his clothes, dusting him with fine grains of sand. It was nearly dusk.

"Watch closely, Arnion," Elyon had said, taking his hand.

A clump of sand churned as tiny heads and flippers began poking out, all covered with glossy black scales. Slowly, the baby turtles wriggled free from the sand and struggled to crest the lip of their nest. One little hatchling flipped himself over in the attempt.

"Can I help it, Father?" young Arnion asked earnestly as he watched it thrash about, trying to right itself.

Elyon put his hand on his son's head and ruffled his hair.

"The hatchling will be all right, Arnion. Remember how we've talked of perseverance?"

"You mean not giving up even when something is very hard."

"Yes, my son."

The hatchling righted itself and began crawling up the edge of the nest, only to flip over a second time. Arnion watched the little turtle eagerly, wishing it strength. Elyon smiled at his son.

"Why is perseverance so important, Arnion?"

"If the hatchling doesn't persevere, he won't make it to the sea."

"Yes. But why should he want to go to the sea so badly?"

"Because he will be able to swim and find food and be with his family."

"Even though the sea has many dangers?"

"Well, if he stays here, he won't be able to live at all."

"Very good, Arnion."

The hatchling righted itself again and, propelled by furious energy, scaled the lip of the nest. Arnion sighed in relief as it joined its brothers and sisters waddling happily toward the surf.

"Perseverance is important for us too. Right, Father?"

"Indeed, perseverance shapes who we are and teaches us to hope."

*Teaches us to hope*, Arnion thought, blinking the memory away. In his spirit, he felt the gentle presence of Elyon.

<Thank you for reminding me, Father.> Arnion sent through his spirit.

He could feel his father's smile in return.

<Take heart, Arnion. In your darkest hour, a light will shine forth and lead you unto victory.> Elyon's words echoed in his son's mind.

Arnion stretched his shoulders and cracked his neck. It was time to get to work. He followed the ambling crowd, coughing from the dust kicked up by thousands of feet. Fragments of gray slag crunched underfoot. He watched as they each found their way to their designated work areas. Some hefted crooked pickaxes and began chipping away at the walls of kelsum stone. Others appeared carrying buckets filled with the jagged gray chips littering the floor. These buckets were deposited into wooden carts pulled by the most miserable-looking people Arnion had ever seen.

He picked up one of the pickaxes that was propped up against a large boulder and moved to a space along the quarry wall in between two other men.

"Good morning," Arnion said lightly.

The man on his right shuddered and turned farther away. The other on his left grunted something but didn't stop from his work, chipping away at the wall.

"Why are we doing this?" Arnion asked them.

He didn't really expect an answer. Every day, he had asked those around him why they kept chipping away at the walls of kelsum.

*Why did Lucien have them collect all the broken chips and have them carted away? What was the point?*

So far, he had been met with grunts and shrugs. No one met his eye, and most seemed content to blatantly ignore him.

The man on Arnion's right cringed and turned away at his words. He was a young man, not much older than Arnion himself. His stubby growth of hair was so coated with kelsum dust that Arnion couldn't tell what its true color was. The young man's eyes were wide, and sweat trickled down between them, dripping off his nose and chin. He kept peeking back at the guard's hut every few minutes and continued his strikes in a frenzy every time one of Lucien's agents appeared in his line of sight.

The other worker on Arnion's left was an older man. The lines in his face and the tiny tufts of white hair on his knuckles betrayed his age. At Arnion's question, the man gave him a sidelong look. After a moment of intense scrutiny, reminiscent of the times his childhood instructors had made Arnion recite ancient Eirenian ballads perfectly from memory, the man shook his head with a sigh.

"What does it matter? Lucien has ordered it, and here we are."

"But what use are all these chips of kelsum stone to him?" Arnion asked.

"Mayhap he uses these stones mixed with mortar to build up his wall. Or mayhap he is lookin' for a way to break men's spirits."

"By making little rocks out of big rocks?"

"Yes." The old man made a grimace and stopped for a moment to wipe the sweat from his brow with a dusty sleeve. He sighed, revealing a mouth with only a handful of rotten teeth.

"Or mayhap Lucien is searching for something." He spat from the gap between his teeth. An arc of grayish saliva sailed beyond them to land a few feet away. Shrugging, the man turned back to the stone wall. "Don't know what ye'd hope to find out here..." His words trailed off in a wheezing cough.

Arnion thought for a moment. *Was there something Lucien wanted from this wasteland? Or was he just using the quarry as a tool to break and dehumanize these people?* "I'm Arnion," he said, holding out his hand.

"There's no need for names in here, boy," the man grunted at him.

"Oh, Dral! Will you two shut up?" the younger worker on the right spoke in a harsh whisper. "This is the kind of stupidity that gets you selected for the weekly spectacle." Shuddering, he resumed his enthusiastic but unskilled assault on the wall of Kelsum stone.

Arnion whistled and leaned against the wall with a grin. "You don't have to worry about them for a while. They're all sleeping."

"How can you possibly know that?" the young man snapped.

"Because they do it every day at this time," Arnion replied. *Sometimes, with a little push from my spirit*, he amended internally. "Listen. If you're quiet, sometimes, you can even hear them snoring."

The older man barked out a laugh that was rusty from disuse. "Yer a sharp one. I'll give ye that," he chuckled.

"Suicidal idiots!" the worker to the right hissed under his breath.

"So, Arnion, is it?" the older man rumbled. "I suppose I could tell ye that I used to be called Has before I came to Gehenna."

"Has," Arnion repeated. "It's a strong name."

"I once was a strong man," Has replied. "But soon, I will die here, as is my fate."

"Why can't you be released once you've paid your debt?" Arnion asked.

"No one ever pays off their debt," the younger man snorted. "Between the interest Lucien charges and the fees for your food and water each day, we all end up owing him more than we could ever work off, even in three lifetimes." At his sudden loquaciousness, Has and Arnion turned toward him in surprise. "What?" he said defensively, averting his eyes. "It's common knowledge."

The prince raised his eyebrows at Has, who gave him a noncommittal shrug. Seizing this rare opportunity afforded him, Arnion tried to draw out his companions more. "He charges you for water? But surely you could just make it yourself. There are many natural deposits around here to work with."

"And how would we do that?" Has asked, leaning a heavy fist against his hip.

"With your spirit. Like this."

Arnion took a deep breath and focused inward. He could feel the mineral deposits in the stone. Arnion walked along the kelsum wall, trailing his hand along it.

"Here."

There was a good buildup of hydrozone he could convert. Placing his hand firmly against the wall, Arnion tapped into his spirit. He thought of water trickling through a streambed, trickling through the stones around him. Pushing the idea outward, he expelled a deep breath through his mouth and felt his spirit pulse through the rock.

Hefting his pickaxe, he struck the wall where his hand had rested once, twice, three times. Then he motioned with his hand for them to approach. Water bubbled out through a crack in the rock.

"We're going to be killed for this," the young man whined.

"I don't believe it," Has gasped. "Ye really did find water." He cupped his hands together, catching the flow in his palms and brought it to his lips. "I've never tasted water like this in Gehenna."

The other worker's eyes widened. With a groan, he too cupped his hands and took a drink. "It's delicious." Laughing, he splashed some on his face. "I suppose this could be worth dying for in such a godforsaken place."

Wiping his hands on his tattered pant legs, he met Arnion's gaze. "Telling you my name won't make any difference now. I'm Eril," he said, extending his hand.

Arnion grasped it tightly. "Eril, it's a pleasure."

The prince's gaze shifted to the flow of water. "This is just a small deposit. It won't last long. Where can I get a cup to share this water with the others?"

"The guards must have something in their hut. I've heard them eating and drinking inside," Eril replied. "But it would be a death sentence to approach them."

Arnion grinned. "They're sleeping, remember? Besides, I won't be long. I'm just going to borrow a cup for a bit."

Eril sighed heavily and grabbed his pickaxe, returning to work. Has gripped Arnion's shoulder.

"Thank ye for the water, Arnion. I'll not forget it." Lumbering back to his station, he surreptitiously watched the strange young man's progress.

Arnion felt in his spirit that the guards were still sleeping. He walked with determination over to their hut, a rough lean-to built into the side of the quarry's wall. Loud snores emanated from inside. Slowly, he pushed open the corrugated metal door. Two guards were slouched over a table, fast asleep. Arnion crept toward them. He could see a large clay pitcher in the center of the table and a cup turned on its side. Red liquid had spilled onto the table and was slowly dripping onto the floor. Judging from the smell, he would guess it was a fairly potent mixed wine. Another cup had fallen out of one of the guard's hands and broken to pieces on the floor. Hardly daring to breathe, Arnion grasped the cup quickly and backed out of the room as softly as a shadow.

Eril and Has both let out a sigh of relief as they saw Arnion emerge from the hut and move swiftly away. Eril shook his head in disbelief, and Has grinned at him.

Arnion moved back to the spring and rinsed out the cup before filling it again with clean water. If something as simple as water could be a gift to these people, he would give it gladly.

A flash of blue eyes caught his attention. Arnion smiled. It was that girl again.

# CHAPTER 4

Acadia dumped her buckets of kelsum fragments in the pushcart and then glanced around quickly for guards before stopping to wipe the sweat off her brow with the back of her hand. She could feel grime sticking to her face and the back of her neck. Her throat burned from breathing in quarry dust all day, and her skin itched from the heat rash blossoming from her knuckles up to her wrists. Acadia scratched at it furiously as she walked away from the cart, drawing blood.

She was so consumed with trying to alleviate at least some of the itching that she walked into someone standing in front of her. Acadia might as well have walked into a boulder. The other person didn't give way at all. As Acadia recoiled back a step, she stumbled.

"Careful," a gentle grip steadied her.

Her eyes flashed up, and she jerked her arm away. *Oh no.* It was that lunatic again.

"I thought I told you to stay away from me."

"Hey, you bumped into *me* this time."

Acadia scowled. His nonswollen eye was crinkled up in a crescent. He was actually smiling. She couldn't remember the last time she had seen someone smile, certainly never in Gehenna unless you counted the serpentine smirks of the guards when they did something particularly cruel. *Not that his smile is particularly pleasant to look at,* she thought as she appraised his disfigured and peeling face.

"I didn't get your name earlier."

"And you won't." She crossed her arms in front of her chest. "No one uses names here. It's meaningless."

"Not to me."

She shifted her feet warily.

*What was with him?*

Acadia tilted her head, examining him.

The young man was as dirty and scarred as the rest of them, and yet he stood straight. He didn't slouch and wasn't afraid to look people in the eye. Acadia had learned early on to avoid eye contact as much as possible. It helped to avoid conflicts with the prisoners around her as well as the conflict within her as she watched others suffer, sometimes at her own expense.

Tearing her gaze away from him, she focused on her throbbing hands and resumed scratching.

*What was the point in thinking about it?*

She needed to get back to her station and get away from this troublemaker before the guards noticed her loitering. Acadia started to walk around him when he held something out to her. It looked like a grimy clay cup.

"Wait, before you go," he said earnestly, taking a step toward her.

"Why would I want this battered old rubbish?"

"Not the cup," he chuckled, smiling down at her again. "Here."

He sloshed the contents slightly. Acadia's throat pinched, and she was suddenly acutely reminded of just how thirsty she was.

"Is it..." She licked her chapped lips and smothered the spark of hope in her chest.

"Water." He nodded.

Acadia snatched the cup out of his hand and peered into it. It appeared to be a cup of water just as he said. Using both hands, she raised the chipped clay to her mouth, intending to take a cautious sip. Once the cool liquid touched her lips, however, she found she couldn't stop taking great gulps until the cup was empty. It had a pleasant earthy taste. All the debtors were charged exorbitant prices for Lucien's recycled water though it was still so filthy that you had to strain the sediment out with your teeth.

"It's time to go," he said as he slipped the cup back from between her fingers. "The guards will be awake soon, and I've got to return this first."

She stared at him, mouth agape. "The guards? You took this from the guards?"

"I borrowed it while they're sleeping." *And judging from those snores, I probably could have ignited a small det blast in that shack without them waking.* He remembered the spilled wine. *Definitely.*

"Take it back!" Acadia thrust the cup away from her. "Getting caught with this would be suicide."

"It's all right. I'm not worried about a couple of guards."

"Not worried? You do realize who they all report to, right?"

"Yes."

For the first time, his sanguine expression faltered. A darker emotion flickered across his face briefly. Before Acadia had a chance to analyze it further, it was gone, seeping from her grasp faster than trying to cup water in her open palm.

"Well, go on." She put her hands on his back and gave him a shove in the direction of the guard's hut. "Return that thing before they notice it's gone, preferably without getting yourself killed."

"All right."

His grin was contagious. Acadia had to bite down on her lip to keep her expression neutral.

"Until next time." The young man tipped an imaginary hat at her and began his uneven stride toward the hut.

Acadia shook her head.

*He is definitely unhinged.*

Yet she found herself hoping that he would survive the encounter and that they would have a chance to talk again. Maybe she was losing it too? Talking to him made her feel a little lighter as if an invisible weight on her shoulders that had lessened slightly.

*How long had it been since I've actually talked to anyone? Could it have really been since the ride into Gehenna?*

She thought back to that day when Lucien's reckoners had come for her.

# CHAPTER 5

Acadia could still picture that fateful morning clearly in her mind. It had been a beautiful day in Beulah. Sunlight filtered through the sheer scarlet curtains, accompanied by the sounds of the city just beginning to wake for the day. She had been sitting at her burled satinwood dressing table still wearing her plush turquois bathrobe. Cira had drawn a warm bath earlier that Acadia had enjoyed without a second thought. Absentmindedly, she was now contemplating the tiny colored glass bottles on the vanity.

*Which fragrance should I choose today? The warm sandalwood in the dimpled red bottle? Or the fresh essence of jasmine flower in the hand-blown glass decanter with the golden cap?*

The large oval mirror on the table reflected the tinted bottles back at her, and she smiled at how the light played through all the different colors and angles. Beside them was her set of matching starlet shell earrings and necklace that she had carelessly tossed the night before.

Suddenly, a strange man burst into the room, shattering the placidity of the morning. Behind him, Acadia could see her maid-servant, Cira, protesting loudly, only to be shoved further out of the way by another exceedingly large brute.

"Sir, I am not yet dressed. I demand you remove yourself at once!" Acadia stood angrily and pointed toward the door. She wanted to sound fierce, but her voice quavered a little at the end.

The man was inordinately large with a large hooked nose and greasy black hair that hung to his chin.

"I'm no more a sir than you a lady."

His tone was snide. She was repulsed by the black rings of rot around his gums when he spoke. Bucephalus took pride in the disgust he instilled in others.

"Whatever business you believe you have with me, it can at least wait until I am properly clothed."

"Can't wait," he grunted. The man stuck a finger in his ear, wiggled it around for a moment, and then withdrew it to examine its contents. "I've got three more to pick up after you and Lucien's terrible set on punctuality, especially with defaulters." He wiped his finger on the side of his ominous black cloak.

At the word defaulter, Acadia's eyes widened, and the hair stood up on the back of her neck. Despite the balmy summer morning, she felt goosebumps prickling along her skin.

"Defaulter? Me? That can't be. I just spoke with Mr. Kinu last week about my accounts."

"You're three weeks past the deadline. Unless you've got fifty thousand drakka hidden under that robe, you're comin' with me."

"Fifty thousand? That's impossible! The agreement was for twelve."

"You're forgetting borrower's fee, interest, and late penalties." Bucephalus's sneer was caustic.

"There's got to be some mistake. I can make the payment. I can sell…" Acadia gestured frantically around the room. "Anything. I'll sell everything in this room to pay back what I owe."

"Your time is up. I've got orders to take you back to Gehenna to work off your debt, and I never miss a pickup. All that's left is to see if you'll come quietly or not," he said, rubbing his grimy hands together.

Acadia could feel the tears burning behind her eyes.

*This couldn't be happening. It just wasn't possible. How could Lucien have sent his reckoners after me?*

She had never felt such belonging, such contentment, until she came to Beulah. She had friends here. Surely, someone would be willing to help her or at least loan her the money until she could pay everything back.

"Just give me a few hours. I have friends here. They will help me pay this ridiculous claim." She wrung her hands in despair.

"Looks like it's going to be the hard way then." Bucephalus tilted his neck to the side, cracking it.

"No, please. You don't understand. If you just give me a little more time…" She circled behind her dressing stool, terrified.

"Times up." He spat out the words like venom and lunged at her.

She dodged to the left, but he managed to grab ahold of her right sleeve. Desperately, she pulled away. There was a loud tearing sound as the exquisite garment tore in the man's grip.

Acadia made a mad dash for the doorway, heaving herself through as she sobbed. Suddenly, she was thrown back as a stinging blow rocked across her face. She fell with enough force that her teeth clacked together painfully as she hit the ground. Acadia lay on the polished wooden floor, stunned. Her ebony hair splayed around her.

Another reckoner stepped out of the shadows just beyond the doorway. Acadia could hear Cira crying quietly behind him.

"Please," Acadia whimpered reaching out to her.

The handmaiden turned and ran in the opposite direction down the hallway.

"Nice catch, Andreas." Bucephalus had followed her out of the bedroom, tossing the sleeve of her robe on the floor. "Everyone always tries to run," he said, shrugging.

Andreas grunted.

"Please," Acadia whispered again.

Tears and mucus were running down her face. She could already feel her cheek swelling from the force of Andreas's blow.

"Why doesn't anyone ever pick the quiet way?" Bucephalus asked as he picked his way over Acadia's tangled limbs.

Andreas merely shook his head and stooped down to grab Acadia by her hair, dragging her up as the girl let out a shriek of pain. She tried to kick out at him, but he just lifted her up higher till her toes scrabbled along the floor and a burning pain seared her skull.

Acadia wanted to keep screaming, but the agony of being pulled by her hair stole all the air from her lungs. Andreas yanked her through the lavishly furnished rooms, and she tried to find some kind of purchase to stop his relentless pulling. As they crossed the threshold into the street, she made a grab for the doorframe. Her nails clawed at the polished molding, and for a moment, she thought she might be able to break free. But then her fingers slipped off, and she was out in the street. As the three entered the more public setting, Andreas released his grip on her hair and instead took her elbow firmly in his grasp.

Onlookers hurried past, their eyes averted, as Andreas yanked the young woman in torn nightclothes toward an unassuming brown wagon. It stood on four mud-splattered wheels and had neatly fitted slats over the windows. Two mottled gray sagrins stood in front, their striped hooves pawing the dirt. As Acadia was dragged toward them, one of the beasts tossed its leathery head at her. Acadia drew back in alarm. Its pupil and iris were a milky white.

Bucephalus drew a ring of keys from inside his coat pocket and fitted one into the lock on the back door. "I guess I do prefer the noisy way after all. Doing it all quiet-like wouldn't be half as much fun, would it, Andreas?"

"Uh-huh." Andreas picked his nose and flicked the brown crust off his finger unceremoniously.

The instant the door was unlocked, the reckoner thrust Acadia up and shoved her through the entryway. The force of his shove was so great that she went tumbling headfirst and nearly did a somersault across the carriage floor. Catching herself on her hands and knees, her body throbbed from the jolt of another blow. The carriage door was slammed behind her with a resounding clang, and she felt her heart stutter.

Small bars of light shone through the slated windows, casting Acadia in a striped shadow. She put her face in her hands and wept.

The carriage creaked and swayed for a moment as Bucephalus and Andreas clambered onto the driver's seats. There was a shout of "Ha!" followed by the crack of a whip, and the hackney took off at a rapid pace.

Acadia sobbed until she had no strength left to weep. Her breath came in little hiccups now, and her shoulders were still shaking with the muscle memory of her tears. Gradually, she became aware that the carriage had simple wooden benches bolted to each side. There on the farthest right-hand corner, enveloped in shadows was another passenger.

It was a portly man. His elbows were resting on his knees, and his head was bent over. He was wearing a nicely tailored shirt, but it was ripped in places. On one of his feet was a glossy black shoe. The other only wore a stained stocking with a hole in its heel.

"Sir, please you've got to help me. There has been a mistake." Acadia crawled over to him and put a hand on his knee beseechingly. The man jerked away.

"I think I'm going to be sick," he whispered, clamping a hand over his mouth.

Acadia backpedaled to the other corner of the carriage. Wrapping her arms around her legs, she rested her chin on her knee and shut her eyes tight.

*This can't be happening*, she repeated over and over to herself like a mantra.

Throughout the day, there were more stops, more shrieks, and more tears as others were thrust through the lighted entryway into the semidarkness of the carriage interior. At one point, the man in the corner vomited. The sour stench filled the small space, and all the other passengers pressed against the slated windows in the hopes of breathing one of the fleeting wisps of fresh air that passed through.

The last to be admitted was a beautiful young woman with shining auburn hair. It had once been in an elaborate coiffure, but through whatever trauma occurred before her entry, it now drooped onto her shoulders, a frazzled mess with loose strands hanging from her neck and sticking up at odd angles from her head.

As the girl sobbed quietly, Acadia was filled with a sudden compassion.

*That was me only a few hours ago.*

She reached out and took the girl's hands in hers. "It will be all right. This is only temporary. We just have to work off what we owe, and then Lucien will release us."

"Do you really believe that? People call Lucien the Heartless King. They say it's because he eats the hearts out of his victims to stay young." The girl turned her tearful stare up to meet Acadia's eyes.

Acadia patted her hand gently. "That's just an old wives' tale. There's no way he would eat us when we still owe him money."

She tried to laugh at her lame excuse for a joke, but it came out as more of a sob. Shaking her head to ward off her own panic, Acadia cleared her throat and willed herself to speak in a calm, controlled voice.

*I can convince her. I'm an expert at this. Just think of it like another job.* "Besides, all those rumors about eating hearts, there's no way that could be true. No one lives forever," she said firmly.

"My great-grandmother warned me about him when I was young."

The petite redhead rubbed her hands along her arms as if suddenly chilled. Her bloodshot eyes burned into Acadia, and the older girl couldn't look away.

"When I was very young, before she passed, Grandma took me aside one day and warned me. 'Beware the demon with eyes of jade. He comes to snatch greedy children from their families.'" She waggled a finger just as her grandmother had done.

Acadia resisted the urge to pull her hands away from the other girl's sweaty grip.

"That doesn't mean it was Lucien. He would have to be hundreds of years old. I've met him. He may age well, but he's definitely not *that* old. It's just a dumb rumor."

She smiled in what she hoped was a soothing way.

The other girl leaned back against the wall of the carriage as if the weight of everything that had happened finally sunk in all at once. She raised her eyes to the roof, dolefully.

"I know it sounds crazy. But I've never seen anyone with eyes like Lucien's before."

"His eyes," Acadia murmured. *I had never seen eyes like that either. They were so unusual. They drew me in. Eyes like magnets, making you a thousand promises without ever actually saying a word. Eyes that make you think you're the only one in existence, that someone finally understands you. He made me feel so precious. What a fool I've been,* she realized, furious.

Acadia vigorously shook her head to clear her thoughts.

*I should have known better than to trust in something as unreliable as another person.*

She looked down and realized that unconsciously, she had clenched her hands into fists. Forcing her hands open, she slid them down the bedraggled fabric of her dressing gown, smoothing out the wrinkles as best she could.

*It's already ruined,* she thought ruefully. *I don't know why I'm bothering.*

But old habits and familiar creature comforts die hard. Looks had been such an important part of her life these last three years. Acadia found herself dying to look in a mirror and fix her hair.

*My face must be a fright,* she realized. *All splotchy and pink. If only I could get my hands on some pashir shell powder.*

Her thoughts caused her to consider the girl sitting next to her again.

*Maybe she has some,* Acadia thought hopefully.

The redhead in question was staring at her hands vehemently, tears flowing silently down her cheeks.

*Or maybe not.*

Acadia resisted the urge to sigh. She didn't like clingy girls, but it had been a terrible day for everyone, so she tried to muster up some more empathy for her fellow prisoner.

"What's wrong?" Acadia asked quietly.

"I've never had to work with my hands before." The girl stammered, turning her soft palms toward her gentle voice. "I don't know if I'll be able to do it."

Acadia squeezed her hands lightly. "Of course, you will. I'll help you. We can stick together."

"Do you promise?"

"I promise." Acadia smiled. "I have a good luck charm that will keep us safe." She tugged at a small gold chain that was around her neck. In the center was a bright red stone. "It's from my home before

I moved to Beulah. I've never taken it off, and it has always kept me safe."

"Oh." The girl breathed.

"You ignorant little fools." Another voice spoke up derisively from the shadows. "Don't you know that no one has ever left Gehenna alive? No pathetic little trinket is going to help you where we're all headed."

It was an older woman dressed in violet robes. Her striking black hair was streaked with gray. She had not entered with sobbing, but in a stately stride. Hoisting herself into the carriage, her eyes blazed with a cold rage. No one had dared approach her, so palpable was her fury, and Acadia suspected that the reckoners had not laid a finger on her either.

Choosing to ignore the older woman, Acadia met the girl's eyes again.

"We can do this. Especially if we stick together. I'm Acadia. What's your name?"

"I'm Delilah."

Acadia smiled at her. "It's a beautiful name."

"Thank you," the other girl said shyly.

After those brief words of tentative friendship, their conversation withered away. Acadia tried to think of something encouraging to say, but the words died in her throat. As much as she didn't want to admit it, that older woman had rattled her. It couldn't be that no one ever paid their debt. Otherwise, Lucien would never have gathered such esteem and regard. Everyone spoke of how generous he was and how willing he was to help others at his own expense.

Acadia propped her elbow on her knee. Maybe she could try to get some rest before they arrived. She leaned her left cheek into the palm of her hand and immediately drew back with a wince, the sudden pain reminding her of the slap she had received earlier. *I'd forgotten about that.* Her cheek was tender. She gently used her fingers to probe the extent of the injury and discovered a painful swelling from her left cheekbone just under her eye to the upper left-hand side of her jaw.

*Come to think of it, Lucien sent the reckoners after me without warning. There must have been some mistake, some misunderstanding or clerical error that landed me here instead of Mr. Kinu's elegant little office downtown.*

Acadia reminisced. Lucien had always been so good about communicating, sending polite little notes checking in on her, making sure she was satisfied with the arrangements. He never mentioned repayment when they spoke.

*It was almost a taboo to talk about money,* Acadia thought. *I did my job, he was pleased. Everything seemed to be going so well. Where did I mess up?*

She shifted her balance and propped her right cheek in her hand instead. Her unwilling companions must also have been deep in contemplation for the rest of the ride passed in a strained silence. Mercifully, their noses even became accustomed to the pungent odor tainting the air. The route got sufficiently bumpier as time wore on.

*We must be outside the paved city streets now.*

Dust kicked up by the wagon's path found its way in through the window slates, making everyone's noses itch and eyes sting.

After what seemed like an eternity in that small dank box, the carriage ground to a halt. They heard Bucephalus call out, "Open the gates! I've got a fresh load of defaulters for Lucien." Even his voice sounded strained.

The cry "Open the gates" was echoed by various other voices in the distance. The passengers could hear heavy chains rattling outside, and a deep rumbling reverberated around them as a heavy wooden drawbridge was lowered. Slowly now, the carriage passed through, followed by the shrieking metallic screams of a portcullis lowering behind them. Delilah gripped Acadia's hand tightly. Acadia squeezed back.

There was a foul odor of sulfur and something worse in the air. Acadia couldn't identify what it was then. The smell of corpses rotting in the courtyard while awaiting disposal was still unfamiliar to her at the time.

The carriage came to a halt, and all the passengers sucked in an unconscious breath. This was the final stop. The lock snapped open, and from the entryway, a torrent of light and sound sliced through the stillness inside.

"All right, out you go." It was Bucephalus smirking at the door. "It's time for processing." He waved toward the cacophony outside.

Acadia slipped out, followed closely behind by Delilah. She brought her hand up to shield her eyes from the sudden brightness. Along each side of the carriage was a line of guards. Their raucous jeers filled the air.

"Hey, you filthy defaulters!"

"Thought you could escape repayment, did you?"

"You bloated pigs! Lucien is gonna bleed you dry!"

Each guard held a taunt metal chain wrapped tightly in their hands. At the other end were snarling ungalors almost as tall as the guards themselves. Long, shaggy hair began in a yellow ruff around their necks fading to a darker brown or black along their back. Their hairless legs stretched out, long and gaunt, tipped with sharp, yellowed claws that raked the gravel in anticipation. Their faces were canine in appearance, with black lips peeled back to reveal elongated fangs. The creatures snapped at the defaulters as they walked past.

One of the guards let his chain run slack, smirking. His ungalor rushed at the man who had been sick, seizing his ankle in its powerful jaws. There was a sickening crunch, and the man let out a bloodcurdling scream.

The guard grabbed up the chain and gave it a ferocious jerk.

"Get back, you stupid animal."

But the beast would not release its hold on the man. Jerking the chain again, the animal was dragged backward pulling the man off his feet, still screaming.

"Someone, please help me!" the man sobbed.

"Aw, shuttup! You could stand to lose a few pounds, you scummy snot-rag."

The guard began beating the creature's head with his fists, but it still refused to let go.

"Tedik, you idiot! That one's not going to be able to work now."

"Aw, sure he will, Tychus. Now, hand me that bolt stunner."

Tychus walked to the wall and picked up a long, black pole with metallic prongs at one end. He handed it to Tedik, who pressed the ignitor switch, sending crackles of red electricity dancing up and down the prongs. Jamming it into the ungalor's neck, the creature spasmed and clamped down even tighter. The man's screams died off sharply as he began convulsing too, electricity passing from the ungalor's jaws into his body.

"Well, look at that."

Tedik laughed and switched off the stunner. The ungalor whined and finally released the man's ankle, now a mess of flesh and bone. It slunk down behind the guard and laid down. The man's face was ashen. His eyes were rolled back into his head in a faint.

Acadia and the others stood horrified, unable to comprehend what they had just seen. Delilah had both her hands clamped around Acadia's right forearm, squeezing so hard her fingers were turning white.

"Welcome to Gehenna," Tedik leered. "Now, keep walking!" He jabbed toward an open doorway ahead.

Acadia flinched and started ahead briskly. It took effort, but she was able to close out the memory of the man.

*The only thing I need to worry about right now is getting myself out of here,* she thought to herself.

Two guards appeared through a side entrance and began dragging the unconscious man toward it. Acadia didn't look back.

In processing, people in dark-blue smocks with slicked back hair observed as they were stripped of their clothes and examined from head to toe. The observers went back and forth between each defaulter, eyes hidden behind reflective goggles. They recorded every article of clothing and every ring and hair clip collected on dark-blue clipboards in elegant silver script. The defaulters were poked and prodded. Measurements were taken of their waists, the set of their eyes, and even the condition of their teeth. Everything was recorded in spidery writing.

Guards entered through a second doorway and forced each defaulter to kneel down on the white-tiled floor.

"Are you going to kill us?" Delilah squeaked out, her vocal cords strained with dread.

Their heads were forced down, and then there were rough scissors in their hair, ripping and tearing without pity. Acadia bit down on her lip and closed her eyes as swaths of her ebony hair fell softly around her like snow. Next to her, she could hear Delilah whimpering. The snipping of scissors gradually stopped only to be following by the brutal scraping of a razor across her scalp. Acadia dug her nails into her palms to keep from crying out. Delilah was sobbing openly now.

When it was all over, Acadia opened her eyes and saw the floor littered with the hair she had once taken so much pride in. So much time was spent applying precious oils or searching out which hairpins perfectly brought out the blue of her eyes. Now all her hard work was made utterly meaningless in the face of this new reality.

One of the observers stepped forward. Her bland face was unexpressive. In a voice without inflection, she repeated as she had hundreds of times before, "Lucien believes in equality. In the utopia that is Gehenna, everyone will look the same, and everyone will be treated the same. There is no partiality. There is no status or wealth. We are all his servants. We exist to only serve him."

She thrust out her hand palm up, like a spear, in a gesture calculated to maintain listening comprehension by eighty-five percent. The glassy-eyed stare of this latest batch of recruits didn't look particularly promising. Mentally, she shrugged and went on.

"Lucien demands absolute loyalty. The penalty for failing him is excruciating death. Serve him and live, or fail him and die. The choice is yours." She extended her hand outward, somewhat magnanimously, she thought, considering the zombielike nature of her audience.

The observer adjusted her glasses so that the glare reflecting back on her listeners was proven in ninety-eight percent of cases to be highly ominous.

"You will leave all vestiges of your past behind for the betterment of the commonality. Pleasing Lucien is all you need to think about now."

Delilah was still crying quietly. Acadia nudged her gently with her left shoulder. When Delilah looked over, she lightly tilted her head down and opened her left palm slightly, hand facing away from the guards and observers. Inside, her lucky red stone glimmered in the light. Delilah's eyes fixated on the jewel.

She sprang to her feet and pointed at Acadia, screeching, "She has something! She's kept something!"

Acadia's eyes widened. She spluttered, "What? No, I—"

"Look in her hand! Just look! Look! I'm loyal to Lucien, I swear!"

The guards who had pushed Delilah back down at the start of her hysterical shouting now turned menacing gazes on Acadia.

"You sneaky little piggy. Give it here."

"I don't have anything, I swear—"

Before she could even finish her sentence, one of the guards hit her in the back of the head, Hard. Acadia fell on her hands and knees when another guard kicked her in the stomach. She felt as though all the air had been squeezed out of her lungs. Bile rose up in her throat. She tried to contain it, to swallow it back down, but it pushed against her mouth insistently. Acadia vomited on the floor.

"Disgusting vermin." It was the observer's monotone. "This is why you all must be cleansed." She kicked Acadia in the ribs, causing her to fall on her side. The observer crushed her boot against Acadia's left forearm, causing her to cry out. "You will relinquish everything."

Acadia squirmed under her boot but didn't have the strength to pull her arm free. Her side and head ached from the blows. She couldn't think clearly. A guard came up and pried open her left hand, picking up the jewel and golden chain with a pair of tweezers as if it was contaminated.

"No," Acadia breathed softly. She was struck again, and she blacked out.

When she had finally come to, Acadia had found herself dressed in a coarsely woven gray shirt and loose pants. She was inside some kind of holding cell. At first, she thought she had been brought to a prison, but later, she learned that these were the sleeping quarters of all Lucien's servants, all those who now owed him their lives.

*I always thought I was so clever that I could talk my way out of anything. It turns out I was never very clever at all.*

Blinking, Acadia shook away the cobwebs of the bitter memory and focused again on the now familiar sights of Gehenna's quarry. It was one of the many recollections she tried so hard to forget.

*Here. Now. Pick up your tool. You can do that. Now, walk back to your station. You can do that.*

The mindless swinging was muscle memory by this point, and it helped her clear her head.

*Rescue,* she scoffed to herself. *The only escape from here is death.*

# CHAPTER 6

Visio ports throughout Capital City were swarming with activity. Ever since Prince Arnion had left on his ambassadorial mission, Eirenian surveillance of Gehenna had tripled. Analysts and their teams of grid screen technicians, messengers, and logistics staff were working around the clock to keep up with the information flow. Each status report Arnion sent through long distance spirit communication was met with a frenzy of enthusiastic scrutiny.

As the closest visio port to Gehenna, station E-6 was running at recon level 8, high alert. The Lead Analyst for the station was young, but she had displayed such a command of her duties that she was promoted quickly through the ranks. Naileah didn't like to think of herself as a prodigy even if that's how others sometimes referred to her.

*I just see the links in the pattern,* she thought.

This was her first time functioning as the Lead Analyst during an ambassador's mission to Gehenna, and she was determined to do everything right. Daily reports were rigorously examined for potential risk management factors. So far, all of her outcome predictions and mitigations had been spot-on.

Sifting through the data collected by her minor analysts, Naileah focused much of her time on the movement and activity of the guards.

*Once they become aware of his presence, things could escalate very quickly.*

She sighed and switched the view on her data pad to the latest grid screen images captured by her technicians on third shift.

*So far, Arnion has done a fantastic job of keeping his mission discreet.*

The irradiated spectrum images were able to display spirit activity that would otherwise be invisible to the human eye. Zooming in and enhancing the images, Naileah couldn't help but be proud of the crown prince.

*He's the real prodigy. Look at how delicately he casts that web of protection around the people he interacts with. It hardly gives off any trace. I doubt even Lucien himself would notice it without irradiated spectrum lenses.*

She zoomed in to examine the image more carefully. Her short, bobbed hair fell forward as she leaned over the device, partially shielding her face from view.

*Just as I suspected. It's not your basic shield either. This has subtle distracting suggestions woven into it. Those guards must start feeling inexplicably sleepy the moment they glance over.*

Naileah highlighted the image and sent a copy to the central database folder. Using her stylus, she tapped out a quick note of explanation to accompany it.

All indicators still looked favorable for success of the mission. Arnion was slowly but surely making headway with the populace as well. Naileah was about to jot down another note in her small neat handwriting when she heard one of her grid screen technicians groan in frustration.

It was Argo at grid screen 3. He roughly jammed down the pause button on his display.

"Argh, I just can't believe these people."

Tilting his chair backward, he ran his fingers through his thick dark hair, agitated. On his grid screen, Acadia's image was frozen as she finished mouthing the words, "I thought I told you to stay away from me."

"They're so disrespectful!" Argo whined. "Do you realize who you're talking to, foolish girl? The Crown Prince of Eiren. He could squash you like a bug!"

Naileah frowned and quietly placed her data pad down on her desk. She cleared her throat loudly and could feel the eyes of E-6's staff on her, waiting to see how she would respond.

"Argo, might I have a word with you?" Her tone was light but clearly not a suggestion.

The technician powered down his screen and stood, face turning red. "My apologies, Lead Analyst. It won't happen again."

His look of self-reproach was so sincere that Naileah briefly considered letting him off the hook with a warning. All of her staff had been tense lately. It wasn't just Argo.

*Whatever resentment he's carrying is likely shared by others in our unit. If I don't stop to address this issue now, it's just going crop up again later on and could distract us at a crucial moment.* Analysis concluded, Naileah refocused on the technician before her. His eyes were staring holes into the floor, fists clenched at his sides.

She stepped over to his side and lightly placed a hand on his arm. "The crown prince doesn't need us to defend his honor. He's more than capable."

The technician took a deep breath and his hands relaxed. "It's just," he spoke in a small voice, eyes flicking upward from the floor to meet her gaze. "Sometimes, I wonder why we keep sending people over there. Is it really worth it?" Argo shrugged his shoulders.

Patting his back a few times, Naileah encouraged him. "Of course, it is! Anything we can do to stop Lucien is worth it. You know that ever since the Fall, we have been losing influence all throughout Elorah. The Deceiver is actively working to turn the other nations against us. Where we once had flourishing relationships with all of them, now we have distance."

She smothered the urge to cross her arms or look away. *I must reassure them that there is hope and a purpose in what we're doing. In spite of how it seems, not all is lost.* Wrapping confidence about her like a cloak, Naileah kept her gaze level with his.

"The crown prince knows this. That's why he's over there risking his life at this very moment. He has compassion on those people. And he needs our support."

Naileah made a sweeping gesture encompassing everyone in the room. "All of us. Prince Arnion volunteered for this mission, and I'm going to help him see it through to the end. The last thing he needs is us bickering over here among ourselves." She lifted her gaze to scan the expressions of the other E-6 staff, face alight with fierce determination.

The tension in the room seemed to leak away like a deflated balloon. Nodding their heads, some technicians stood for a brief stretch or rolled their shoulders with a sigh. One analyst cracked his neck loudly, eliciting chuckles from those nearby. Everyone turned back to their stations with renewed conviction in their hearts. Lead Analyst Naileah was the glue that held them together. Her loyalty reminded them that if their prince thought something was worth fighting for, they would stand by him.

"Thank you, Lead Analyst." Argo smiled at her. Holding together the middle and index fingers of his right hand, he touched his heart and then his forehead in the traditional Eirenian gesture of solidarity.

With a slight nod, Naileah repeated the motion back.

*That seemed to clear the air*, she thought, satisfied.

As she turned to pick up her data pad, one of the messengers called out to her.

"Ma'am, we have just picked up a spir-com with status update relayed from the crown prince. I am forwarding it to you now."

"Thank you. Please direct copies of his spirit communication to the other analysts as well."

Naileah tapped the message open with her stylus. Arnion's update was brief and to the point.

> *Beginning to make headway on primary mission. Still unclear whether Lucien is deliberately searching for something or just using the quarry as a tactic for extreme subjugation. Will continue to investigate as a secondary objective.*

As copies of the prince's latest report circulated the room, E-6 began to buzz with activity once more. Naileah could feel a renewed energy coursing through her staff.

*Couldn't have come at a better time, Your Majesty*, she thought to herself. Clapping her hands, she said out loud, "All right, everyone, you heard the crown prince. Let's get to it."

# CHAPTER 7

Arnion sighed deeply, exhaling. He was sitting cross-legged in the gravel a short distance from the holding cells. After sending a status update to Eiren, he sent a brief personal message to his father. It was early, so early the night had not yet relinquished its hold on the sky. Breathing out slowly, he released the taunt pull of his spirit and felt his connection to Eiren fade quietly into the background of his thoughts. Elyon's presence was still there, faintly tugging at the back of his senses, ready to be called upon if needed.

Arnion had woken up early to walk with his father for as long as he could remember. Sometimes, they walked through the palace gardens, other times along the gleaming white battlements or in the rolling hills beyond the castle walls. Before most of the palace staff even began to stir, Arnion and Elyon had completed one of the most precious parts of their day.

Being a ruler was a difficult, time-consuming job. If it weren't for their walks, days might go by without father and son finding time to spend together. The constant needs of the kingdom were always pressing down on them. It was always a challenge to make the distinction between what seemed urgent and what was truly important.

In Eiren, citizens mastered the skills of long-distance communication via spirit during childhood. Although it was a common and frequently practiced skill, most people still preferred to be materially present with one another when possible. Arnion was no exception. He thought of his father's quiet steps along the path, the sure way he walked, and the twinkle in his eyes when they recounted some childhood mischief. Arnion opened his eyes and straightened his shoulders.

Dawn began to break over the hills, and a splash of light crept over the gray landscape. Arnion stood, briefly considered attempting to shake some of the dust from his clothes, and then shook his head chuckling.

*They're only going to get dirtier.*

As he walked toward the kelsum quarry, he heard the screeching of two kraggies fighting. They snapped and clawed at each other, trying to tear at a scrap of flesh. Arnion turned away in revulsion. It was a human hand.

He saw the line of prisoners making their way through the piles of aggregate to their work positions. Remembering the two men from the previous day, Arnion retraced his steps.

*Has and Eril.* He smiled. *The first two people in Gehenna in whom I've seen a shred of breakthrough. There was that girl too, the one with the blue eyes.*

A smile tugged at the corner of his mouth. *She tries to come off as callous and indifferent, but her expression is always conflicted as if she's fighting against herself.* He rubbed his chin thoughtfully.

*Or as if she's forgotten who she truly is. Is this just the result of living in Gehenna? Or had she already forgotten long before coming here?*

The intensity of his own curiosity surprised him. *She's really quite fascinating,* he thought to himself.

Snapping his focus back to his immediate surroundings, Arnion noticed that Has and Eril had left a space for him between them. He hefted his pickaxe up onto his right shoulder and walked over to them.

"Good morning, my friends."

"Will you be quiet," Eril seethed through his teeth with a whispered breath. "Or we'll all be beaten by the guards."

Arnion looked at Has, who gave a slight nod toward a wiry-looking guard standing to their right.

"That un's nasty," he mumbled as he chipped away at the stone.

Arnion turned to face the rock wall as well. "I'm sorry," he whispered.

Has favored him with a grunt and turned back to his work. Eril ignored him completely, chipping away at the rock wall with vigor.

*So much for progress with the locals.*

Arnion sighed and shifted his pickaxe to his left arm.

*This truly is work that could break a person. The repetitive monotony is almost worse than the backbreaking labor. What is Lucien after, having us work out here all day long? The advisors and analysts are all convinced Lucien is building an army, but it appears as though all he's doing was working his prisoners to death. What was the point? Most of the people here are far too weak to mount up an attack against anyone, least of all a technologically advanced country like Eiren. What's his real motive?*

Arnion pondered as the hours wore on, sweat dripping from his brow and trickling down his back.

*I need more information.*

Arnion was just beginning to contemplate how to strike up a conversation when Eril mumbled something in his direction, eyes still facing the quarry wall.

"How did you do that, finding water yesterday? I've been thinking about it all night."

Arnion smiled. "I didn't find it. I made it using my spirit."

"Made it?" Eril stared at him open-mouthed for a moment before flinching and turning back to his work. "That's impossible. It must be some kind of trick."

"No, my friend. I wouldn't deceive you. Where I come from, it is basic knowledge taught to all children. A good survival skill."

"Where ye come from?" Has echoed softly but said no more.

Arnion could tell the older man was curious, though his eyes remained fixed on the wall of kelsum in front of him.

Eril stopped chipping away at the stone and angled himself toward Arnion once more. "So if this is some simple child's game, anyone should be able to do it?"

"It's not a game, but yes, with the right training, anyone could do it," Arnion replied.

"Would you teach me?"

"I would be glad to."

Arnion put forward his right arm. Eril hesitated for a moment before taking it, but then he gripped it tightly with a slight smile before letting go.

Arnion rolled his shoulders, exhaling a breath. "The first thing you need to do is relax and calm your spirit."

"My…spirit?" Eril said skeptically. "What is that? Some kind of magical force?"

Arnion rubbed the bridge between his nose and his brow for a moment with two fingers. "No, not magic. It's your spirit, who you are. Your inner self."

"Like a soul," Has piped up.

"Yes!" Arnion met the older man's bright gaze with a grin. "You have a physical body inhabited by your spirit. When we die, our body stays here, but our spirit moves on."

Eril rolled his eyes. "This is all very fascinating theology, Arnion, but I don't see what it has to do with making water from a rock."

Arnion put his hand on the wall of kelsum before him. Closing his eyes, he exhaled slowly. He spoke quietly, and his mind focused elsewhere.

"Our spirits are more powerful than you can imagine. With it, I feel through the stone, searching for a pocket of hydrozone deposited many thousands of years ago when these minerals were pressed together in the depths of Elorah." He trailed his hand lightly along the wall. "Here! There is a small pocket, just enough for a cup's worth."

Eril raised his eyebrow, staring at Arnion.

"Here." Arnion grasped Eril's hand, placing it where his had just been. "Feel it here. The hydrozone has a sort of electric tang compared to the blandness of the kelsum around it."

Eril pressed his palm into the rock, closing his eyes. After a moment, he opened them.

"I can't feel anything," he said, shrugging.

Arnion frowned. Children in Eiren were taught early how to tap into their spirits. It was central to life. They would never be able to access a fuga or even a low-speed trilorid hovercraft without decent spirit focus. *What's blocking him from sensing it?*

"May I?" Arnion asked, hovering his hand over Eril's.

Eril sighed and gave him a skeptical look. "If you think it will help."

Arnion sent a small tendril of his spirit into Eril, searching. He could sense Eril's spirit curled deep inside him, a tight little ball of light-blue energy. From the way it was so tightly bound, Arnion could tell he had never tapped into it in his entire life. He exhaled deeply. Arnion didn't want to hurt Eril or scare him with an overwhelming surge of energy all at once. Perhaps if he just gently nudged Eril's spirit, it could work itself out of the bindings around it. Arnion pulled back all but a needle thin wisp of his spirit. Very gently, he used the tiny thread to tap the outer layer of the bindings within Eril. Instantly, it flared up a deep bright blue with pale flaming arms like a brindle star.

"Whoa! What's happening?"

At Eril's alarmed cry, Arnion pulled back completely. As he did so, he felt Eril's spirit returning to the passive blue little ball.

Eril's gaze was fixed on his hand against the rock wall. The hair on his arm was standing straight up. Small chips of kelsum that had begun spinning in a miniature vortex around the young men fell to the ground suddenly with a gentle tinkling.

"Are you all right?" Has clamped a rough hand on Eril's shoulder.

"No... I mean, yes, I'm fine. Nothing's wrong. It's just..." Eril ran a hand over his cropped head, releasing a puff of gray dust. "For a moment, I felt this intense energy flowing through me." He put his hand back on the wall. "I could swear for a moment, I felt a tang in the rock, like you were describing Arnion."

"The hydrozone." Arnion placed his hand on another spot on the wall. "Once you've located it, it just takes a simple nudge to alter the molecule structure from a mineral form to a liquid. You get fresh, clean water."

"But how did you...how did I feel it for a moment?"

"It felt like your spirit was sleeping deep inside you. I just gently nudged it awake."

"So I can access that energy again?"

"It will take practice strengthening your ability to tap into your spirit. Just like any muscle, it needs to be exercised."

"Incredible." Eril breathed, flexing his hand.

Suddenly, a loud gong sounded throughout the quarry.

"Lunch." Has grinned at them. "Better hurry!" He rested his pickaxe on the wall of kelsum and began jogging over to the southern wall of the quarry.

"Hurry, Arnion, or there won't be any left." Eril was already moving quickly toward the wall, but he turned back and gestured at Arnion to follow. "You really are hopeless."

Arnion smiled. At least Eril was showing some concern for his well-being. That was a step in the right direction. He shuffled after his new friends as quickly as his limp would allow him.

There were a handful of guards along the southern edge of the quarry wall. Each carried a dirty sack, which they were reaching into and tossing loaves of bread down into the scrabbling hands of the crowd below. The people were screaming and tearing at each other desperate to get a bit of nourishment.

"Once they run out, that's it." Eril was next to him, panting. "You have to be aggressive." A roll sailed toward them but fell short in the crowd. "We need to get closer," he whined and began shoving his way further into the squirming mass of bodies.

Everything was chaos. The undercurrent of sobbing was pierced by inhuman barks and yells. Arnion's stomach roiled as he watched. Next to him, a man with a pockmarked face seized a hand that was grasping a roll and bit down hard, drawing blood. The roll dropped to the ground and was crushed as the two men fought bitterly.

The prince had no intention of fighting with others for a scrap of bread, and yet he found himself caught up by the swell of people around him. He was unwittingly carried forward toward the front, when something bumped against his foot. Arnion inhaled before looking down. But it was only a roll, hard as a rock and beginning to show small spots of green mold. He picked it up, attempted to dust it off against his filthy shirt, and then, smiling at the futile gesture, pocketed it. Arnion turned, calculating how to best extricate himself from the frenzied crowd when he felt a hand clamp around his ankle.

"Help me," a faint voice rasped

Arnion whirled around quickly and looked down. He was horrified to find an elderly woman, bruised and bleeding, being trampled by the crowd.

# CHAPTER 8

The old woman's lip was split, blood dripped from her chin, and she had a nasty gash that was turning into a bump on the right side of her head. She tried to say more, but her words were swallowed by a cry of agony as she continued to be crushed by the crowd.

Immediately, Arnion bent down and scooped up the frail creature in his arms. She was so thin it felt as though her bones were made of matchsticks. Arnion cradled her against him, shielding her from the blows of the crowd that was still frantically fighting among itself. Gradually, he got her to the fringe of the commotion and set her down on a small boulder.

"Are you all right?" he asked her gently.

The woman was sobbing quietly, shoulders shaking. Tears were caught in the wrinkles of her face, making erratic trails down her cheeks.

"I'm so hungry," she moaned. "I've always been able to snatch a crust before, but today, I lost my footing. Before I knew it…" She shuddered and began weeping again.

"It's all right. You're safe now," Arnion soothed.

"It's not the crowd," the woman mumbled, wiping at her tears. "It's me. I'm too old to survive here any longer. I have seen the starving ones, too weak to catch their meals. It is not a good death."

Arnion put his hand on her shoulder. "If you let me, I would like to help you." He pulled the roll out of his pocket and held it out to her. "I'm sorry, it's a little dusty."

She took the roll with trembling hands. "You don't even notice the dust after a while. Probably feel strange without it crunching between my jaws now."

Letting out a rueful chuckle, she asked, "Why are you so eager to give up your bread to another prisoner?"

"I am a visitor here."

"A visitor to Gehenna? Never met one of them before." The old woman eyed him cautiously. "You're not a guard, not a reckoner, not a defaulter?" She raised her eyebrows at him.

Arnion met her gaze unflinchingly. "No."

The elderly woman sighed and began pounding her shoulder with a chopping motion. "Agatha doesn't mind meeting a visitor, but there are others here who will. Be careful who you tell."

"Thank you, Agatha. I will."

Agatha grinned at him, a gaping smile missing several teeth.

"Please, let me bring you more bread tomorrow. Don't go back into the crowd."

"If the visitor wants to give Agatha his snack, what's to stop him?"

"Exactly." Arnion's face took on a serious expression. "I will make sure you get your daily portion."

Agatha placed a gnarled hand over his. "Such a kindly visitor. How can an old goat like me ever thank him?"

"It's Arnion."

"Arnion." Agatha squeezed his hand for a moment before letting go to tear into the roll with both hands.

Acadia kept toward the back of the crowd. Although more food was always snatched up by those at the front, the savvy waited near the back. There was no sense in getting crushed by the mob when a little patience was usually rewarded with less effort. The naive newcomers had energy. They would force their way to the front and be some of the first to grab a morsel of whatever rotten food the guards were tossing out that day. Gleeful and overconfident, they let themselves be carried toward the back where hungry eyes sized them up.

*Here comes one now.*

A burly man, scalp still red from processing, shouldered his way to the rear. He laughed to himself, clutching three rolls to his chest. Turning to sneer at the crowd behind him, he never noticed the leg that snaked out to trip him. As he tumbled to the ground, he was set on by three scrappy youths.

Although less than a third of the man's size, the children were quick. Armed with sharp kelsum fragments, the urchins methodically stabbed at his eyes, hands, and legs. Bellowing, the man lashed out at them. But his aim was off, probably owing to the blood now impeding his sight.

Acadia watched the whole scene while creeping forward slowly, shielded by the piles of rock. As soon as the brute was distracted, she abandoned her stealth and sprinted toward him at full force. Sliding to a stop just inches from the fray, her cloud of dust further added to the confusion. Acadia snatched one of the discarded rolls and placed it in her pocket. One of the children noticed what she was doing and leapt at her with wild eyes. He tried to grab her ankle, but she kicked him away and took off at a quick jog. Acadia was careful not to move so fast that she couldn't look out for legs or other traps laid out for the unwary.

After traveling about a quarter of the way around the swarming mob that was still grubbing for food, Acadia was satisfied that neither the youths nor any other pursuer was following. She sat down on a large boulder and drew her legs up to rest her head on her knees. Acadia watched the crowd listlessly, but her ears were still alert to the sounds around her and the possibility that someone still might try to sneak up behind her.

A strange movement from the crowd caught her eye. It looked like someone was being carried. People died in Gehenna every day. Family bonds and friendship were broken quickly. You either learned that no one else was going to save you at the cost of their own comfort and safety or you died. Acadia's heart thrummed. She had never seen someone be carried out of the lunch riot before.

The young woman blinked, shocked to feel tears forming at the corners of her eyes.

*How stupid! What am I getting sentimental about? It's just a waste of energy. Why am I even watching?* She scratched at the rash encircling her wrist like a blistering red bracelet but couldn't resist sneaking another glance upward.

*Kindness here only prolongs suffering. It'd be more merciful to just let the weak die quickly.*

And yet the man's actions, for she could see it was a man now as he made his ways toward the edge of the crowd, caused a fierce ache to bloom in her chest.

Others turned to stare at him incredulously as he made his way through. He was quiet, navigating around the writhing throng without throwing so much as a single punch or kick to clear his way. Shaking their heads, the people around him quickly forgot the passage of the strange man and his burden as their stomachs rumbled, and they turned their faces once more toward the fray.

Acadia slid off her perch and swiped roughly at her eyes with the back of her hand. She couldn't believe what she was seeing. It was her lunatic carrying an elderly woman in his arms.

*Of course*, she thought to herself, *it would be him.*

She watched from a distance as he lumbered to a gray rock about knee high, his gait hindered by his limp. The man set the woman down gently.

*They seem to be talking now*, Acadia frowned to herself. *But what could they possibly have to talk about? You don't just strike up conservations with someone you might be in a life-and-death struggle with tomorrow. It makes things unnecessarily hard.*

The young man's blatant indifference to his own survival grated on her. He continually acted in a way that guaranteed his own swift destruction. Yet she found herself deeply curious Acadia clenched her fists and took a deep breath.

*I'm being ridiculous. Still, what could it hurt to know?*

She already had her meal saved for later, and at least this would be a novelty from watching the multitude tear itself apart.

Acadia discreetly began making her way closer to the unlikely pair. She felt her jaw drop when the man reached into his pocket and gave the old woman his roll.

*What is he thinking? Does he really want to die so badly?*

They continued to talk, the old woman placing a hand over his. The cries and shouts from the crowd were beginning to lessen, but it was still much too noisy for her to catch their conversation without getting close enough to spit. Acadia bit the corner of her lip. *Maybe this was a bad idea after all.* One second later, she knew it was a bad idea as the young man smiled at his companion and began walking away, directly in her path.

*Curse me and my curiosity! I should know better than this.*

Acadia thought about her options. She could melt back into the crowd and forget about this stranger. Then she remembered seeing how gently he carried the old woman. Acadia felt an indescribable longing in the depths of her marrow. She had to know more about this strange man. If that made her crazy too, so be it. Maybe he wouldn't even remember her.

Acadia planted herself in front of him, hands on her hips.

"Ahem," she coughed loudly.

Arnion's eyes brightened. "Oh, it's you again."

He smiled at her. The rash still swelled on his face, making Acadia want to cringe. So he did remember her.

She huffed and gave him her most steely-eyed glare. "Why did you do it?"

Arnion scratched the back of his neck. "What, the roll?" He tilted his head slightly to the side and raised an eyebrow at her.

Acadia stomped her foot. "Any of it. The roll, the carrying. Anyone else would have just left her there." She wanted to shake some sense into him.

Arnion looked at her seriously, smile fading away. "One day of hunger won't kill me."

Acadia averted her gaze. Nudging the dust with the toe of her shoe, she mumbled, "That's a sure way to a quick death. There's always someone in desperate need around here. You won't survive long if you keep handing out all your food."

Her arms fell to her sides, and she nibbled her bottom lip. Before she could think about it further, she reached into her pocket, drew out her roll, and broke it in half.

"Here." Acadia thrust the larger half into his hands but refused to meet his gaze. "One day of hunger won't kill me either." She sighed. *Apparently, lunacy is contagious.*

"Thank you."

Arnion's eyes were wide. He knew what it meant to give up the chance for nourishment in this place. He looked off into the distance for a moment deep in thought. Then he considered the young woman in front of him, who had just offered him something precious. Resolution settled over his face.

"Hold out your half."

"What? Now you want the rest?" Acadia scoffed. She wanted to take a step back but forced herself to stand her ground.

"No," Arnion chuckled. "Just trust me."

Acadia eyed him warily.

*Was this some kind of trap?*

But she had offered him the roll of her own free will. He had no way of knowing she would do that. She remembered his hand leading her away from the guards, giving her fresh water to drink, and carrying the old woman. She met his serious gaze and pursed her lips wryly. Slowly, Acadia held up the other half of the roll toward him.

Arnion lifted his right hand so that it was hovering slightly above hers and closed his eyes. Exhaling slowly, he reached into his spirit. Geometric patterns of burning white electricity began to trace their way along the roll's surface. After a moment, they focused on the edges, sparking furiously. Acadia watched, unable to breathe as the roll seemed to knit itself together again out of thin air. In just a few seconds, she held a perfectly complete roll in her palm while the stranger still grasped half of the original in his own hand. She flinched as a final wave of light crackled around the now whole roll in her hand and then vanished.

Acadia shivered. She looked at the roll in her trembling hand and then back at the young man.

"W-what just…how did you…" Her voice trailed off.

"People don't use their spirits much here, do they?"

Arnion lowered his hand back to his side. He took a large bite out of the half roll in his left hand so that it puffed out the right half of his mouth while he chewed.

"Spirit?" Acadia's voice came out higher than normal.

Arnion swallowed. "Another time." He took another crunchy bite. "We've got to go," he said with his mouth full.

Arnion turned and headed back into the crowd. The guards were now funneling everyone back to their stations in the quarry. The crack of whips and the thump of bludgeon sticks echoed off the walls.

Acadia stared after him as he made his way through. The man must have felt her eyes on him because he glanced over his shoulder at her, waved with his last bit of crust, and then continued walking away. She focused her attention on the roll, raising it up to her eyes for inspection. It looked—fresh. Acadia broke it in half, surprised that it ripped apart softly rather than cracking open with staleness. She could swear that she even saw a small waft of steam escape from the middle. The roll was warm.

Cautiously, she tore off a small piece. It was so fluffy that it seemed to melt on her tongue. Acadia even tasted butter as she swallowed. The guards never threw away anything fresh. It was always moldy, putrid, or barely edible food. Sometimes, it wasn't even edible, and then everyone was wracked with torturous stomach cramps or worse for the rest of the day. There was no way that this was the same roll she had stolen earlier.

Not one to look a gift horse in the mouth, she ripped off another piece and savored it for a moment. The bread was delicious. The delicate texture was addicting, and within seconds, she had devoured the whole roll. She licked her fingers as she joined the crowd trudging back to their workstations.

*I must finally be losing it*, Acadia decided.

She grabbed her pickaxe and headed over to her section of the quarry wall. After a few moments of pounding at the rock to loosen small chips of kelsum, Acadia licked her lips. She could still taste a trace of butter.

# CHAPTER 9

"You look happy."

Eril swung his pickaxe over his left shoulder as Arnion joined him at the wall. Arnion rolled the handle of his pickaxe between his hands and met Eril's gaze.

"I am. I think I made a friend."

Eril sighed deeply, shaking his head. He hefted his tool over his head and brought it down against the rock wall, muttering something that sounded suspiciously like "Hopeless."

"Ye like her, don't ye?"

Has glanced at him out of the corner of his eye while he continued to work. Arnion laughed and ran a hand over his prickly shaved scalp.

"I never said it was a she."

Has grunted, but it sounded suspiciously like a chuckle. "I may be old, but I'm not *that* old."

Arnion laughed and nudged him with his shoulder. "Very observant, Has."

"A she? Oh, Dral! You can't be serious?"

Eril smashed his pick hard enough into the wall that it stuck there suspended. He turned to face Arnion. "She'll turn on you the first chance she gets. You can't trust anyone in here."

"I can trust her." Arnion let the edge of his tool rest against the ground for a moment, handle leaning against his leg. "The same way I know that I can trust the two of you."

Eril gaped at him. He stuttered, trying to work out some argument against Arnion's clearly delusional optimism. Finally, he closed his mouth and shook his head, giving up with a shrug of his shoulders.

"You really are a strange one, Arnion."

Arnion laughed and clapped him on the back.

"Not as strange as you all seem to me."

"Speaking of strange," Has mumbled, "it's a bit odd how the guards never seem to take notice of us when yer around, Arnion."

"Coincidence, old man." Eril wrenched his pickaxe out of the wall and resumed his chipping at the kelsum. "Either that or Arnion's blessed with some kind of fool's luck."

"Probably luck." Arnion winked at Has.

Eril coughed. "I'd like you to show me once more, Arnion. That spirit thing. I think I can get it."

"Of course! I would be glad to." Arnion put his pick down and turned to face Eril. "Show me what you've got so far."

Eril put his palm against the kelsum and closed his eyes. He drew in a slow deep breath. Sweat trickled down his neck. He tried to remember that feeling of electricity traveling throughout him. He cleared his thoughts and focused on the rock in front of him. Bland and gray, it felt the same as always, but there was a slight buzz to his right. Without opening his eyes, Eril began tracing his hand along the wall. As his hand traveled downward, he bent his knees to continue following its path. Kneeling, he could feel a sort of tingling beneath the stone. Something was different here. He could feel it.

"Arnion, here! There's something different. I can sense it." Eril kept his hand on the spot but twisted so that he could glance at his friend. "I can't believe it. I can really feel it."

Arnion bent down next to him and placed his hand on the stone.

"Let's see. Yes, you're right. There's a good-sized deposit of hydrozone here." He clapped his hand on Eril's back. "Well done, Eril! Now, the next thing you must do is nudge the hydrozone with your spirit, compelling it to change its form."

"Compel it?" Eril took his hand off the wall. "But that…how can that be possible?" he trailed off.

Arnion bent his head closer to his palm and breathed out. He felt his spirit flowing through him and into the stone.

"Once you get used to it, using your spirit is just like breathing."

Arnion's spirit flowed through the hydrozone. Beneath the rock wall, molecules sparked and fused. Drops of water condensed into the pockets of the stone, growing larger and larger until the cache contained about a liter of liquid where the stone had once been.

"Here, Has." Arnion took a small shard of kelsum and scratched a mark into the wall. "Once I return with a cup, would you do the honors?"

Has halted his chipping and wiped the perspiration from his brow with the back of his arm. He met the young man's gaze.

"I will." Has glanced away toward the guard's shack. "Be careful, Arnion. It's not a game to them."

"Thank you, my friend. Don't be troubled. The guards here have no authority over me."

The older man grunted and turned back to his work, clearly unconvinced. Arnion chuckled and turned toward the guard's hut.

Acadia gripped the wooden handle of her pick tightly and brought the metal point down on the gray stones again and again. She kept playing the memory over in her mind.

*What happened back there? It was impossible. Who is that man? What is he?*

*Slam!* The pick came slashing down again. Bits of kelsum flew in the air. Fragments bit against her skin. Dust ghosted her body like a shroud. She could see him so clearly in her mind, cheerfully tilting his head, his eyes crinkling. But then, she remembered the electricity flowing over the roll, sewing it back together. It didn't make sense.

Acadia hacked at the rocks until she had no strength left in her arms. Panting, she fell hard on her knees. Beads of sweat were running down her back. The kelsum dust stung her eyes. She tried to wipe them with the inside of her damp shirt, but it only served to irritate them further. Coughing, she pulled up the edge of her collar and inspected it to see if it was slightly cleaner.

"Here, try this."

*That voice.*

She lifted her head, settling bleary eyes on him. Sure enough, it was her lunatic. He was holding something out to her. Acadia tried to focus on what it was. It looked like a cloth of some kind. Drops of water were dripping from it, pattering to the ground one by one. The thought of water made her lick her cracked lips.

Acadia snatched the rag from him and gave it a rapid assessment. It appeared to be clean, and a quick sniff revealed no suspicious odors. She pressed the damp cloth to her eyes and tried to smother a sigh of contentment. It felt so refreshing. The itchy stinging feeling subsided, replaced by coolness. She could feel her skin soaking in the water from the rag.

Acadia patted her eyes once more, relishing the feel of moisture on her skin. She tried to press the memory of this feeling deep down into her mind. Then she stuffed a corner of the cloth into her mouth and began sucking on it. There was no sense in letting water go to waste.

"Wait, wait."

Arnion tried to put a hand on her arm. Acadia flinched from under his touch and continued sucking on the cloth. She took a step back. If he tried to take it away, she would make a run for it, guards be cursed. He seemed to read her thoughts.

"I'm not going to take it," he soothed gently. Arnion kept his arm slightly extended, palm out, in a placating stance. "Look, I brought you something to drink as well."

Acadia had been tensing her muscles to flee, but at his words, she relaxed her stance slightly. She took in the metal tin he was holding out to her. Condensation was starting to form along its surface.

"Wha iz ih?" At his puzzled look, she pushed the rag to the side of her mouth and tried again. "What is it?"

"Just water."

"Where did you…" She drifted off as he shrugged at some indiscriminate point off in the distance. "Oh, never mind."

She took the cup and drank from it greedily. It was cool and refreshing. Her throat tingled in satisfaction as she swallowed. The water in Gehenna always left her feeling thirsty, no matter how much she drank, but after a few mouthfuls of this water, she felt inexplicably full and rejuvenated. There was still a little left in the tin. Acadia was tempted to finish it off.

*When will I get another chance to enjoy clean water?*

Her thoughts turned inexorably to the man standing before her, who had shared his bread with a stranger. She reluctantly took her mouth off the cup and, before she could think the better of it, held it out to him.

"Here, there's still a little left." *Dral, I must be crazy to give up clean water like this. What is wrong with me lately? I'm making beginners' mistakes.*

Arnion waved the cup away. "No, it's all right. You can finish it. There's more. We've been sharing it with the others."

Acadia looked up and saw a distant point along the wall where a small crowd was gathering. Two men were guiding the people to form an orderly line. Those at the front bent down and came up with their hands cupped. They appeared to be drinking something coming out of the wall. The faint sounds of laughter drifted toward her on the wind. Acadia had never heard laughter in the quarry before, except the cruel hacking of the guards when they tormented someone.

"What are you?" she asked, uncertainty creeping into her voice.

Arnion held out both hands, palm up. "What do you mean?"

"I mean how can you do these things? It reminds me of when Lucien came to our village."

Arnion winced and took a step back. His hands drifted to his sides, but he kept his gaze fixed on her. "I am not working for Lucien," he said with finality. "I could never serve him."

Acadia released a breath she didn't realize she had been holding. "But you and him, the things you can do are similar."

His gaze burned into her, intensity rolling off him in waves. Finally, he looked away. "I can see now how you might think that way."

In the distance, the other workers continued their backbreaking labor. The muscles in Arnion's jaw tightened. *These people have been lured into a trap with no means of escape.* Anger burned within him. He clenched his fists and took a deep breath.

"Lucien uses his abilities to deceive and oppress others. He has become consumed with hatred and pride." Arnion relaxed his grip and looked up at her again, crestfallen. "Is that really how you see me?" he asked quietly.

*Dral, am I actually feeling guilty?*

"No, I don't," she said.

Acadia's stomach fluttered as his expression seemed to lift slightly. She tapped her fingers against the cup.

"It's like you remind us how to be human again." She finished off the water in one large gulp and wiped her mouth with the back of her hand. "Thank you."

She held out the cup to him. This time, he took it. Their fingers brushed briefly, and he smiled.

"You're welcome." He held out his hand to her. "I'm Arnion, by the way."

After a breath of hesitation, she took it. "Acadia."

"It's a beautiful name."

She dropped his hand like it was on fire and glared at him. "You! You really aren't a prisoner here, are you?" she snapped. *Why do I feel self-conscious all of a sudden?* She crossed her arms in front of her chest and jutted out her chin.

His obvious amusement at flustering her only served to irritate her further. Arnion resisted the urge to take hold of her hand once more.

"I told you when we first met. Don't you remember?"

Acadia remembered the leering guards and how they had grabbed her. She could remember the cruelty brimming in their eyes. Then a quiet voice and a steady hand had led her away to safety. She had not forgotten; she had just dismissed it as crazy. Acadia felt a lump in her throat and swallowed.

"I never thanked you for what you did back there, Arnion." *Arnion. My lunatic has a name now.*

"Acadia."

She liked the way he said her name. Arnion took her hand and raised it to his lips.

"I would do it again in a heartbeat." He kissed her hand chastely and looked up at her, eyes sparkling.

# CHAPTER 10

<Sikes, you lazy swine! Remind me again why I put up with you?>

The spir-com reverberated with menace. Lucien paced his office on the third floor of Gehenna's main compound. He paused momentarily to peek through a slat in his blinds and stare at the courtyard.

<Well, Y-Your Majesty, I have extensive knowledge of the customs and peoples of Mintra's mountain tribes. I have been able to negotiate at least a dozen contracts this year alone.> Sikes's spirit communication whispered hesitantly back.

Lucien dropped the slat and rubbed his fingers to his temples, agitated.

<Thank you for reminding me how spectacularly you have been failing in your quotas. My Diamond of Avathys brings in twice as much alone.>

He sent back the spir-com with sufficient force to cause its recipient a splitting headache. Feeling Sikes's wince, Lucien smiled. <Why are you behind yet again?>

<Your Grace, please, have mercy on me.> The broker was desperate. <I live to serve you. Everything I do is with you in mind.>

<You take too long to collect. I've been watching you closely. And you aren't pressing the families enough. When one defaults, you should be pressuring the others to try and take on some of their debt. Familial compassion and all that.>

<Yes, M' Lord. You are absolutely right. I will correct my shortfalls immediately.>

Lucien felt Sikes's humble submission through their spirit connection.

Smirking, the Heartless King turned away from the window and strode toward his desk. <Very good, Sikes. Your obedience pleases

me.> If Sikes had been physically present, Lucien would have stroked his head like a pet ungalor. But Sikes was thousands of stadia away in Mintra. <It reminds me why I've bothered to forge a link with you and the other brokers, why I've bothered to share my considerable power and longevity.>

Lucien sank into his joffa fur-lined chair with a sigh. The furry little creatures were so adorable. Most people in Elorah didn't have the heart to kill them. *But they make such an exquisite lining.* The Heartless King stroked the sleek fur with pleasure.

<I've not forgotten how you orchestrated that plague in the mountain streams. That was very clever, Sikes. We were able to gain a strong foothold in Mintra because of you. But I need more creativity, more thinking outside the box. Can you do that for me?>

<Yes, Your Grace. I will not fail you.>

Sikes's spirit sounded a little stronger now as Lucien relaxed his stranglehold grip upon the broker's mind.

<Good.> Taking out his kelta pipe, Lucien tamped it full on the desk. <I expect you to implement all those changes we've been talking about.>

At Sikes's enthusiastic response, the Heartless King continued.

<I'll be sending some new contracts in anticipation of those family members you're going to start working on, along with an increased ration of ink. Let me know how things progress.>

He severed the connection before he had to listen to more of Sikes's groveling. Sighing, Lucien inhaled deeply of the pipe's aroma-therapeutic herbs.

*Even being connected to those seven brokers is draining. How I long for the day when they are no longer necessary.*

The spirit link Lucien had forged with his brokers did have its uses. Spir-coms were still the fastest and most reliable way for him to pull the strings on his web of informants.

*Not that it was easy training those fools in the use of spir-coms.* Lucien took another long pull of his kelta pipe and sank into his chair. *Still, they have their uses.*

He grabbed the bell on his desk and rang it thrice loudly. There was a knock at the door as a guard begged entrance. Lucien waved him in.

"Tell the scribes to prepare three dozen familial debt contracts for Mr. Sikes up in Mintra. I'll also be preparing an increase in his ink allotment. Have someone in to collect it at sundown."

The guard bowed again without speaking and made a hasty exit.

Remembering his ingenious contracts pleased Lucien. He took a long drag on his pipe and leaned back.

*Those contracts are my magnum opus. Of all my wonderful, twisted creations, and there are quite a few, they* truly are magnificent.

Elorah's contract system was quite complex. It took many years of study to master the subtle delicacies of the law. Lucien had studied well.

*Oh, how I studied them.* He rubbed his hands together, practically purring. *Now, I'm at the point where all the templates I could ever need have already been drafted. A hundred scribes stand ready to reproduce them at my beck and call. It's always "Make me beautiful. Make me rich. Give me power."*

He sneered at the fire blazing in his hearth.

*A little creativity in the asking would be a welcome diversion. Still, the rabble's predictability makes them all the easier to control.*

Curling his toes, the Heartless King stretched luxuriously. He looked down at his nails with a yawn. *I suppose I should get started on that ink, tedious though it is.* Strolling to the fire, he emptied out the contents of his pipe, tapping them into the flames. Their sweet aroma filled the air.

Lucien walked back over to his desk and reached around to the left-hand corner. When his fingers found the circular rosette carved there, he turned it clockwise until he heard a faint creak. A hidden compartment opened along the interior wall.

Lips curved in a smile, Lucien collected three fresh white ink pads along with their hinged cases. He also grabbed the jar of ink solution he had boiled a few days ago and a smaller glass bottle with a rubbery dropper screwed into the cap.

Holding the bottle up to the light, Lucien shook it gently and frowned.

*Nearly empty again.* A fearsome grin split his face. *That means business is good.*

Carefully, he unfolded his penknife, black blade glittering in the light of the fire. He scrutinized the fingers on his right hand for a moment before selecting his thumb and slicing it open with the penknife. Holding the bleeding digit over the bottle, he was careful that not a drop was wasted.

*Too precious a resource.*

His thumb throbbed, and Lucien encouraged the blood flow with his spirit.

*By this evening, you'll never miss it,* he coaxed himself.

The liquid welled thick upon his finger, dripping furiously into the glass. When it was full to his satisfaction, Lucien licked his finger and willed it to knit itself back together.

*Now, onto the ink.*

He filled the dropper with his freshly harvested blood and tapped it gently on the side of the bottle to clear out any air bubbles. Then he carefully added six drops to the ink solution.

*Too much and the contract is too binding on myself. Too little and I don't have enough control over my pets.*

The blood swirled within the jar, seeping through the milky white solution. Within a few breaths, it had turned the contents a vivid crimson.

The contract bindings were twisted just enough to misalign the blood oaths. Without the right wording, Lucien would have fallen under its thrall as well. His artful manipulation of the legal terms, along with the diluted blood seals that his brokers affixed, allowed him to escape all the normal consequences of an Elorah blood oath.

*A weight which I am happy to avoid,* Lucien thought to himself. *Those obsequious brokers are burden enough. I hardly need the pressure of thousands of mindless workers hindering my every step.*

Nestling the ink pads into their engraved metal cases, Lucien applied his newest batch of blood ink to them with precision. Once the ink pads had turned a shimmering crimson, each case was closed with a satisfying little click. He fingered the embossed *L* on the cover, written in an elegant, curling script.

*I still have time to check how they're progressing over in Sector N while these absorb. How lovely.*

Face bright with anticipation, Lucien locked the door behind him.

# CHAPTER 11

Acadia had trouble falling asleep. Normally, she fell like a stone onto the heap of rags in their cell, practically comatose from exhaustion. Tonight, as her cellmates bit and scratched at each other for the tattered shreds of cloth, Acadia sat apart and hugged her knees to her chest.

"Do you ever think there could be something more?" she whispered, more to herself than anyone else.

The scuffling in the room began to die down. The usual victor was again established at her position in the center. The other three girls, backs to her, were sulking at the edges. One sucked at a fresh red gash on her arm with a filthy mouth. She cringed away from Acadia's gaze.

"We don't have to live this way, like animals. Even if that's how Lucien treats us."

The girl stared at the floor with blank eyes. The rags in the center of the room quivered as a strange ghoulish sound began emanating from within them. It took Acadia a moment to recognize the macabre, high-pitched sound for what it was, laughter.

The girl in the center was the same one who had told her she would get used to things in Gehenna. The rags hung from her scalp like lank strands of hair. Her teeth gnashed, and her glassy eyes burned into Acadia's.

"You've cracked," the girl said in a giddy whisper. "That funny man has gotten into your head."

"I used to think he was crazy too." Acadia met her stare even though it disturbed her. "Now, I'm not so sure. Maybe we've all gone crazy, and he's the only sane one left."

This elicited another giggle from beneath the rags. "Crazy gets you killed," she sang out in a syrupy voice.

Acadia clenched her teeth and looked away. *How often have I thought the same myself?* Her arms tightened about her knees, and she rested her forehead on them. *How often have I used that excuse to protect myself at the expense of others?*

She could see Arnion so clearly in her mind, gently carrying that old woman through the stampeding crowd. It was Arnion who took her hand and led her away from those lecherous guards, Arnion who went out of his way to find her and bring her water despite the limp he staggered around with.

*Arnion.*

He was the only good thing she had ever encountered in Gehenna.

Acadia brought her hand up to her mouth, remembering the kiss. She could feel her face heating up and was glad for the darkness.

*Arnion.*

Her mind summoned a final image of him, the shape of his silhouette against the hazy evening sky. Acadia breathed out a sigh and finally drifted off to sleep.

Time passed, and Arnion continued to visit her often. She found herself looking forward to their conversations. It felt like she could talk with him about anything.

Arnion was gaining a following too. People flocked to him. A cynical person might rationalize that it was just because he was handing out water to the prisoners for free. Maybe that was true for some, but Acadia knew that Arnion had some kind of deeper pull. People were drawn in by his kindness and his humanity. She had felt it herself. In Gehenna where people were encouraged to turn on each other like beasts, Arnion's compassion shined like a beacon of hope. Maybe things could change.

*But how long can this really continue before Lucien catches on?*

Acadia didn't want to think of what would happen then. She had tried to broach the subject to Arnion numerous times, but he would brush her concerns aside.

"Don't worry," he would tell her with sincerity. "When the time comes, I will deal with Lucien."

She couldn't press him any further than that. He would clam up like an impenetrable wall.

Acadia still trembled when she thought of the last weekly spectacle Lucien had held. The sound of the dying man's shrieks and the tearing of flesh and bone were burned into her mind forever. The prisoners were woken early by the guards banging on their cells and beating anyone who didn't rise quickly enough. Yawning and rubbing their eyes, the people moved through the hall, gradually being funneled into the courtyard. Dawn had not broken yet. The sky was the color of a vicious bruise that had just begun to fade. Lucien liked to do his spectacles early in the day. He claimed it reminded his citizens to maintain the proper mindset as they worked.

Lights shone on the stage from three directions, but the crowd was in darkness. The prisoners shuffled back and forth on their feet, nervous. No one ever knew what to expect.

Suddenly, Lucien was on the stage. Everyone's eyes were riveted to him. His deadly beauty shone like a serpent with gleaming scales. Lucien had a magnetic quality that drew people to him with trembling and wonder.

"My beloved people," his voice rang out, deep and resonant, "welcome to our weekly spectacle. You know how much I abhor suffering, your suffering in particular." Lucien cupped his hands together and smiled out at the crowd.

"But you are so childish and forgetful that I have to remind you time and again how to behave. Like a loving parent, I always have to step in and correct you." He shook his finger at them now, a rakish smile curling the side of his mouth. "Here I am before you again to remind you of the rules and the consequences should you fail to abide by them." The smile was gone now. "Our participant today is a classic example."

Acadia's heart leapt into her throat. The image of Arnion streaked through her mind.

Lucien continued, "In fact, he flaunts the rules with disdain. It's almost as if he doesn't believe they apply to him."

She could feel her palms sweating. *No, please not him,* she thought desperately. *Not Arnion.*

"He has been stealing from us!" Lucien shouted now. "Not just from me but from you, my pets, for all that I have is yours. Don't I share all that I have with you?" His face molded into a pout. "Have I withheld anything you asked for during our agreements? Why then am I treated with such contempt?"

There was a quiet murmuring through the crowd.

"He has treated me with contempt! And he has treated you all the same. Are we going to allow him to treat us this way?"

Lucien was working himself up into a frenzy, his words coming faster and sharper. The crowd was infected by his toxic energy. People began stomping and gnashing their teeth.

"How dare he treat us with such disrespect? I will not allow it! I, Lucien, will repay him tenfold."

Agitated whispers rose up like a smog in the air. Lucien smiled as he paced back and forth on the stage.

Acadia couldn't bear it. Any moment now, she expected to see Arnion being dragged up onto the stage, forced to suffer through whatever new twisted punishment Lucien had devised. Her stomach roiled within her. Acadia put a hand to her chest and tried to calm her frantic breathing.

*Not Arnion. Please anyone but him,* she silently begged.

"Lestald," Lucien called out, beckoning to the guards off to his right. "Why don't you join us up here, Lestald?"

The guards nodded, and an escort of four more entered the courtyard. They formed a square around a fifth man. The man in the center was shackled hand and foot. Lestald shuffled along weeping. He tried to swipe at the mucus dripping down his chin once or twice, but it was impossible with his hands chained to the iron that bound his feet.

As Lestald got closer to the stage, he dug his heels in the dirt, refusing to go farther. The guards around him laughed and shoved him, but Lestald did not budge. His eyes were wide with terror, and his sobs faded into great gasps of breath. After a moment, one of the guards grabbed the chain around his hands and physically pulled him up onto the stage. Lestald's feet left grooves in the dust as he passed.

"Lestald, my pet, you're looking rather pale."

Lucien pranced up to him, a malicious smirk painted across his face. Lestald's eyes rolled, and he started to fall. Two of the guards caught his arms and forced him to remain upright.

"No fainting now, you rascal."

Lucien slapped him across the face. It seemed to help the man gather his senses. His gaze fixed on Lucien, and he shrank back almost into the arms of the guards.

"We need to see justice done. After all, it's only fair."

"Only fair!" a voice answered from the crowd.

A ripple of agreement murmured through the people.

In the dark, Acadia let out a breath. So it wasn't Arnion after all. Somehow, he had still managed to escape Lucien's notice. Acadia felt her arms shaking and wrapped them around herself tight. It was still going to be terrible for this man, but most of her was shaking in relief. She felt tears prick the corners of her eyes.

"Lestald, will you confess what you have done?" Lucien asked in an affable voice.

The prisoner opened and closed his mouth wordlessly like a fish out of water. Urine began to dribble down his leg.

"I'll take that as a no."

Lucien turned to face the audience. "This filthy worm was found stealing loaves from the kitchens. Your loaves! The very food you live on. You disgust me, Lestald, stealing from your own people."

He turned and spat in Lestald's face.

"Well, no more! I always catch those who seek to harm us. Always." Lucien gave one final sneer at Lestald and turned back to his captive audience.

Some in the crowd looked at Lucien with adoration. They were calling and cheering his name. Acadia looked away in disgust.

"Well, my pets, we can't let him get away with it, can we?"

Lucien opened his hands to the crowd. Hate-filled voices shouted back.

"Thieving scoundrel!"

"Kill him!"

"Death's too good for 'im!"

The grin that split Lucien's face was terrifying to behold. He had the multitude in his thrall.

"Now, Lestald, you will face your punishment. You've eaten your fill, and now, Cassandra will have her fill of you."

Lestald's face turned ashen. He would have sunk to his knees if not for the two guards holding him up. A roar rose up from the crowd. People were cheering, stomping their feet, and gnashing their teeth with anticipation. It was as if the multitude had become a great thrashing beast writhing in the darkness.

Lucien waved his hand, and a door slid open from the side of the courtyard wall. A roar split the darkness, and the agitated movement of the crowd became still.

"Cassandra, my darling," Lucien crooned. "Come up here please."

Out of the darkness in the wall stepped the largest ungalor Acadia had ever seen. Cassandra was pure black from her head to her tail. Even the skin of her hairless long legs was dark, instead of the usual fleshy pink. Her claws raked the dust at her feet, and her midnight eyes glowed with malice. There was no chain connecting her, and as she padded toward the stage, everyone drew back, even the guards.

Making her way through, Cassandra snapped at the people around her, eliciting screams of terror. She seemed to feed on the fear that spread through the audience and licked her lips maliciously with a long, black tongue. Only Lucien seemed unfazed by her.

When Cassandra put her front paws on the stage and pulled herself up, the wood groaned from the strain. Lucien minced up to her, cooing inane little noises.

"Oh, my dear, you are a beauty." He scratched under her chin. Cassandra whined softly and tilted her head to the side.

On the other side of the stage, Lestald seemed to have found his voice. He was screaming. "No, please no. Anything but this. Not like this."

The prisoner began squirming in the grasp of his captors. Desperate, he kicked out at the guards and sunk his teeth into the arm of the one on his left. The guard let go, swearing, but before Lestald could use this to his advantage, the guard on his right hauled back and punched him in the face. Lestald fell to the floor, quivering.

"Chain him up," Lucien commanded. "And let justice be done."

The two guards grabbed Lestald's chains, one of them shaking his injured arm, and secured his leg irons to a metal ring that had been fastened to the stage floor. Lestald sat back on his rear and crab walked as far away from Cassandra as his chains would allow him.

Lucien took two steps back from Cassandra so that he was on the edge of the stage facing the audience. He beamed at them.

Acadia covered her face in her hands. She couldn't bear the thought that this man was going to be eaten alive in front of them. They were all starving here. Any one of them would try to steal food if they thought they could get away with it.

How could they cheer and laugh at this man's death when many of them would do the same? How could they not see it was Lucien's cruelty that was to blame for starving his people?

Hot tears slipped down her face. Acadia didn't even know Lestald. She couldn't remember if she had ever seen his face before, but she cried for him. Great sobbing gasps rose up from somewhere deep inside her. This disdain for human life was truly wicked, and Lucien was at the center of it all.

"Somebody, please, make it stop," she whispered through her tears.

Suddenly, she felt arms wrap around her and draw her close. Acadia tensed, frightened. She looked up and met a familiar gaze.

"Arnion," she whispered.

"Are you all right?" He thumbed away her tears and met her eyes. "I saw you crying."

"I'm all right but that poor man…" Acadia swallowed and looked away. She gripped his shirt tightly between her fingers. "I thought it might be you."

"No," Arnion said softly.

Acadia continued to cry, turning her face into his shoulder. Arnion glanced up at the stage. Lucien snapped his fingers, and Cassandra pounced on Lestald. His bloodcurdling screams filled the air. Acadia started to lift her head.

"Don't look." Arnion turned so that his body completely blocked her view of the stage and tightened his grip on her. "It's terrible."

Abruptly, Lestald's cries were cut off. The crowd cheered and surged forward. Although the people jostled around them, Arnion held Acadia steady. She lifted her head from his shoulder and was moved to see tears in his eyes as well. His gaze, however, had turned steely.

"This cannot be allowed to continue. Lucien must be stopped."

At his words, she felt cold terror course through her veins.

"You can't confront him, Arnion! It's hopeless. This is our life now, our punishment for being foolish and greedy. We all willingly bound ourselves to Lucien, and this is our reward."

She saw in his face a determination that unnerved her. Acadia clutched at his arm. "It's not your fault he died. Please, let it be."

"It doesn't matter whether or not it's my fault." He took his arm from her grasp. A part of him felt angry with her for her complacency. "Something has to be done. Part of the reason that Lucien has been able to progress this far is because no one here has had the courage to stand up to him."

Acadia's eyes grew wide. She heard the accusation woven beneath his words. Arnion instantly regretted it. The people in Gehenna were trained from the time of their arrival to accept their situation as hopeless and that there was no point resisting. He couldn't blame her for being manipulated by the system. Yet she had cried for this man, a stranger to her, while others laughed and cheered with bloodlust at his suffering. Acadia was unique, and he had hurt her.

"Acadia, I'm sorry." He reached out to her, but she hesitated just beyond the range of his fingertips. "Please forgive me," he said softly. "I wasn't blaming you."

Wordlessly, she came back into his arms and hugged him fiercely.

"I know that you're scared," Arnion continued gently, "but I'm asking you to trust me, please." He put a hand on her chin and tenderly turned her face up toward his. "Can you trust me, Acadia, even if you don't always understand?"

Acadia was torn. She had learned even on the way into Gehenna that you couldn't trust anyone here. Yet there was something special about the young man who was now studying her expressions so avidly. Acadia had seen his compassion and experienced his kindness more than once. It defied all the logic she had carefully crafted to protect herself.

*My heart tells me I can trust Arnion, but how can I blindly let go of the rational judgment that's gotten me this far? Not that my position right now is very good, but I'm alive, aren't I? That has to count for something.*

Acadia couldn't bear to meet his gaze any longer. She looked away and murmured, "I'll try."

Still, it was enough to drag a small grin out of him.

"Thank you, Acadia." Arnion's voice was bright, and he kissed the top of her forehead briefly before releasing her. "That's all I ask of you."

He extended a hand, and she took it in hers, stifling the smile that attempted to break through her façade. Fingers entwined, they joined the stream of workers making their way to the quarry for the day.

# CHAPTER 12

Acadia shook herself out of the memories that clung to her like a damp mist and focused again on the present.

*Speaking of Arnion, where had he gotten off to?* she wondered.

After bringing a load of kelsum chips to the cart, her eyes had scanned the walls for her lopsided friend but to no avail. It was just about this time that he or Eril would open up a vein of water from the rock and invite others to join them for a moment of refreshment and rest from their hard labor.

Amazingly, the guards did not seem to take notice of this frequent occurrence, with prisoners slipping away from their duties, gathering for a short time around Arnion. Lucien's minions seemed totally unconcerned and never approached the crowds that gathered. Even their aggression toward the prisoners at other times of the day seemed to dampen.

*Almost as if they'd lost interest in us.*

Acadia's lip quirked. She was sure Arnion had something to do with it although he carefully skirted around the topic whenever she tried to point it out.

*For a man who befriends others so quickly, he sure keeps a lot to himself. Where has he gotten himself off to?*

Acadia noticed a group of three children scampering over a low ridge off to the right. She furtively glanced around, but the pervasive feeling of disinterest once again seemed to have settled over everyone. No one was paid any attention to her or what she was doing. Acadia leaned her pickaxe against the rusted cart and craned her neck to follow the path of the youths. She couldn't see anything beyond the ridge they had climbed over. Her toes crunched in the gravel as she swiftly followed their path.

The slope was steeper than she realized. Acadia found herself using her hands and knees to pull herself up over its crest. She began carefully picking her way down the other side before the view struck her.

*There must be over a hundred people gathered here!*

Those around the outskirts were standing, while those more toward the center were seated. There were men, women, and children all gathered together from different ages and backgrounds. No one was pushing or fighting. There was an amicable silence as they all focused on someone in the center, listening.

*There's Arnion!*

Acadia saw Has and Eril on his right, helping to pass out water to those still waiting for a drink. But it was Arnion's words that held sway, not the water. *What could he possibly be saying to hold them all captivated like that?*

In her hurry to descend, Acadia skidded down the rest of the ridge, a shower of pebbles tumbling behind her. She wanted to get close to him, but the crowd was so big. Nobody was pushing or jostling, but there were so many people. She would never be able to get through. Acadia tried to stand on her tiptoes, just so she could catch a glimpse of him, but it was no use. He was too far away.

"Acadia."

It was impossible that he could have seen her among so many, and yet it was his voice without a doubt. At his call, the crowd parted forming a path right to the center, and she could finally see him. Arnion was smiling at her.

"Come on. I've saved you a seat close to me."

His words stole her breath away as surely as his voice had paved a way through the crowd.

Acadia was stunned. Arnion was so much more than he appeared to be. He was kind and gentle but also a remarkable leader. The people around him had finally taken notice. She knew now that he could have his choice to sit down and talk with anyone he chose, not just in Gehenna but anywhere. Yet here he was, calling out to her. Here at her lowest point, she had found someone who accepted her unconditionally, who genuinely just wanted to be around her. All at once, her throat felt tight, and her eyes stung.

*Dral! I am not going to start crying. Absolutely not.*

Acadia blinked furiously as she made her way down the aisle that had opened to accommodate her passage. As she drew nearer, Arnion sprang up to meet her.

"Acadia, how are you?"

He took her hands in his as he led her to where he had been seated. She suddenly felt shy under his gaze.

"I'm well. And you?" she mumbled.

"I'm well. Better now that you're with us." He winked at her. "I've been waiting for you to get here."

"Not if I got here?" she quipped.

"No, not you." A good-natured chuckle rumbled through him. "I knew that you would find me."

Arnion guided her to sit next to him on an outcropping of rock. Her arm brushed against his as she slid into her seat. They were close enough that she could feel the heat radiating from him.

Acadia pinched the fabric of his sleeve with her right hand. She was still feeling strangely self-conscious. "How did you know I was there?" she asked in a quiet voice.

He turned on the ledge to face her, and his knees bumped against hers. Acadia swallowed. Arnion was looking at her with a thoughtful expression.

"I felt a pull in my spirit, and I knew instantly it was you. I could feel you were looking for me."

"Ah, I see," she trailed off lamely, looking down at her hands.

"Is everything okay?"

*Dral, now I'm making him worried. What is wrong with me?*

She noticed people around her were staring, some with placid smiles and others with a hint of curiosity. Acadia shook her head vigorously. "Yes, I'm fine," she stammered. "Please continue what you were saying."

Arnion seemed on the verge of questioning her further but mercifully decided not to. She was not sure she could account for her behavior even to herself at the moment.

"I was sharing some stories from my childhood. But I had just asked Agatha if she would tell us a story from the time she was young."

*Agatha.*

The old woman sat close to Arnion on the right-hand side. Her feet were crossed at the ankles, and her worn sack-like dress seemed to envelop her wrinkled body like a shroud. In contrast, her eyes sparkled playfully, and she swung her legs as they dangled like a little girl.

"Agatha knows just the one. You reminded me of it, Arnion, with your tales."

She gazed off into the distance, a small smile playing on her face.

"My brother Tel was only one year younger. We were so close, growing up in the mountains of Iylon where the paths through stone were worn smooth by the passage of those who came before. We used to weave little traps with reeds on the banks of the Chuyna River and use them to catch skaklops and crabs. Skaklops are slippery little devils, you know. They can slip right between your fingers if you're not careful. But their meat is so tender. It always made our mother's stews more delicious.

"We would catch them and place their wriggling little bodies into our hip sacks. You had to tie them tight, or the little buggers would slip out through the top." Agatha patted her side as if checking for the hip sack that had once been there.

"Once, when we were about halfway up the stone path, Tel started twisting his leg this way and that. First his right leg, then his left until he collapsed on his rear. I had been following along behind him and rushed forward, thinking something was wrong. When I came upon him, he was laughing, with tears in his eyes. His hip sack had come loose, and his skaklops had crawled into the hem of his pants tickling his stomach and legs. He was so ticklish. It was useless. We had to take off his trousers and shake them out over the bushes. All our catch for the day escaped into the brush, but we just laughed and laughed. Those skaklops couldn't have chosen a better victim. Tel was so ticklish. He would hunch himself into a wee ball, pulling tighter and tighter until you couldn't reach in to tickle him anymore."

Some in the crowd smiled. Others looked wistful. A few of the younger ones squirmed at the thought of so much tickling.

"Oh, Tel and I, we used to have such good times. Always laughing. I had almost forgotten."

Agatha stopped swinging her legs. Her focus was again on the people around her.

"I haven't thought about Tel in so long. Haven't spoken his name in even longer. But I'm glad I could tell you about him today."

Arnion had been watching Agatha with an affectionate expression. She glanced at him, pensive. He nodded at her. It was subtle, but Acadia caught it.

# CHAPTER 13

Agatha took a shaky breath.

"We had lived up in those mountains for so long. Generations of my family, fishing, farming, trading occasionally in town for little trinkets. Nothing important. We relied on the river for so much. But then the water turned bad. Sickness came. People got the fever, the shakes. They would die all twisted up gasping for breath."

Agatha pressed her trembling hands against her thighs.

"First, it came for my parents. I made it through that, somehow. Probably because taking care of the little ones took all my energy. But when it came to Tel, I felt the agony of his every ragged breath as if it were mine.

"Rumor had it there was a trader in town who sold medicines. Some swore he had a powder that could cure fever. I took what little money we had, along with a bundle of malta bound up with string, hoping I could make a trade.

"The town was dusty, ragged from the winds that ripped through the pass. Everything looked ten years older than it was, including the people. Not like our village, at least not before the sickness came.

"The letters on the signs were strange. I couldn't find my way. I had never gone into town on my own before. There was always an adult, someone older, to help me. But there was no one left now. I rubbed the dust off the shop windows to peer inside. Nothing looked familiar. The townspeople scurried by in little huddles, whispering. I didn't realize then, but no one wanted to catch the sickness from me.

"My heartbeat was pounding in my ears. They were all staring at me, and I suddenly found myself terrified. The wind kicked up a cloud of dust, stinging my eyes and throat. I turned to run far away from this strange, fearful place. And that's when I collided with him.

"Mr. Sikes, as I soon came to know him. He was dressed in a fine red suit trimmed with gold. The buttons gleamed in the sun, dazzling my eyes. His hands clamped down on my shoulders gently as if to steady me.

"'Whoa, child, you've got to look where you're a-going.'

"He was the first person in town to speak a word to me, and his eyes were so kind. I started to cry.

"'Tel's sick, and they won't help me. He's going to die, and I don't know what to do.' My shrill cry was half swallowed up by a gust of wind. I stood there, wailing in the street, rubbing my eyes with a grubby fist.

"'Easy, child. Slow down and tell Mr. Sikes once more. Slowly now. Who's going to die?'

"'My baby brother Tel.' I crouched down then. Wrapped my hands around my knees and rocked back and forth like a baby. 'The water's bad, and he's sick with the fever.'

"Mr. Sikes stooped down beside me. 'And that's why you've come to town, child? To try and help your little brother?'

"I hiccupped and nodded.

"'Well you've come to the right place. Old Sikes will get you sorted out straightaway. There's a trader in these parts who has just the thing. You come along with me now.'

"Mr. Sikes extended his hand, and I took it. It took my whole hand to hold onto his index finger. His hands were so big. I clung onto him like he was my lifeline as he led me down the street.

"We passed a few of the windows I had peered in earlier and stopped at a grim-looking building at the end of the row. There were no windows, no sign on the door. I mentioned this to Mr. Sikes.

"'But there's no sign.'

"'Ridell's a strange one. His philosophy is if you don't have the persistence to find his place, you probably don't have anything worth trading.'

"He winked at me.

"'And no windows?'

"'You see, child, Ridell has some very special objects in there. Some can't be exposed to too much light. That's why there's no windows.'

"I nodded my head but didn't fully understand. Standing in Mr. Sikes's shadow, I half hid behind him as he lifted the latch on the door. It was a big, heavy door made of sturdy throllwood planks. It squeaked as it opened, making me jump.

"The interior was dimly lit by oil lamps. They gave off a foul-smelling black smoke. It reminded me of cooking fat.

"'Ridell,' Mr. Sikes called out. 'It's Mr. Sikes here and his little friend. We're here to make a trade.'

"It took a few moments for my eyes to adjust to the near-dark room. Objects seemed to swirl, appearing and disappearing again in the smoke.

"The thump of heavy metallic boots sounded from the back of the shop. Ridell lumbered out of the gloom, in stained overalls, thin circular spectacles reflecting the lamplight. He glared down at me over his dark bristly beard, like I was vermin.

"'Sikes, what have I told you about bringing those mountain rats in here? Isn't it enough that they've brought the plague to our very borders?'

"'Now, now, Mr. Ridell,' Mr. Sikes said placatingly, 'how about we show a little charity? This little un's made a brave journey all by herself just to see you.'

"'Charity?' Ridell scoffed. 'That's not why you brought her to me. Do you know who this man is, little pest?'

"My whole body was shaking. I can still remember how small I felt, squirming under his gaze.

"'He's Mr. Sikes, my friend,' I stammered out.

"Ridell took a step toward me and leaned down, his eyes burning into mine like hot coals. 'Mr. Sikes is no one's friend. He's a broker for Lucien. Do you understand now, brat?'

"'N-no.' I took a step back and grabbed Mr. Sikes's hand.

"'Come now, Ridell. You're frightening the child. And I surely don't know what you mean by that insulting tone.' Mr. Sikes's voice, though friendly, had an edge in its undertone.

"Ridell stood up straight again and met Mr. Sikes's gaze. They looked at each other for a moment silently. Then Ridell looked away.

"'I meant no offense, Mr. Sikes.'

"'Of course, you didn't.' Sikes clapped Ridell soundly on the shoulder. 'But you can't be too careful with your tone of voice. You wouldn't want someone to misinterpret it, now would you?'

"'No, I wouldn't want that,' Ridell answered quietly.

"Mr. Sikes laughed heartily and stuck his hands into his pockets. 'Well, now that we've got that sorted, why don't you see if the child has anything to trade?'

"Finally, something I understood.

"'I do!' I piped up, feeling secure for the first time. 'I have money and fresh malta that I can trade for medicine to stop the fever.'

"Ridell gestured to a stained throllwood counter on the left. 'Put what you have up here so I can gauge what it's worth.'

"I reached into my satchel and carefully began unpacking my things. The malta was fresh, picked from the river. I had carefully wrapped it in silcloth and tied it with string to keep it from turning brown. The coins were in a small beaded pouch my mother had made for my tenth birthday. I carefully laid them out in a row on the counter, in front of the bundle of malta.

"Ridell picked over the coins frowning. He untied the silcloth bundle and grunted.

"'This malta is good quality, and you packed it well. It could make fine scarlet dyes for Beulan robes. But there's not nearly enough here to pay for what you seek.'

"'I can bring more, lots more. Malta grows well by the banks of the Chuyna, and I know where to find it.'

"'I don't take promises for payment,' Ridell said grimly.

"I wanted to cry. Tel was at home struggling for breath, and all my efforts were wasted. Then Mr. Sikes spoke up.

"'Don't cry, child. We don't have to give up just yet. You say you know where to find more of this malta?'

"'Yes, Mr. Sikes. I can find lots more.'

"'Well then, I think we can come to an arrangement. How much will it take for you to give up some of that medicine, Ridell?'

"The trader cracked his neck. 'I won't take anything less than thirty drakka. The plague's already to the edge of town, and people been clamoring for this medicine.'

"'Well, thirty drakka certainly doesn't come cheap. And each bundle of malta is only worth about ten til. But, child, if you bring me one bundle of malta every week, tied up nice like you've done here, and I'll pay for this medicine today. Now, how does that sound?'

"I didn't understand then all the talk of money. I knew that a bundle of good malta leaves could bring in two plucked chickens, a full bolt of cloth, and a couple of fistfuls of candy from the store. It seemed all the wealth in the world to me at the time. I had no concept of what a drakka was or how much it would take to pay Mr. Sikes back. All I could think about was a chance at getting Tel the medicine that would save him. Nothing else mattered to me then. I'd probably do the same today if I had to choose.

"Before I knew it, I had signed the contract with Mr. Sikes in his office. He purchased the medicine for me, and I was walking back to my village in the mountains. The medicine worked quickly, and Tel was soon back to his plucky self, pulling skaklops and setting traps for the small animals that came to drink from the Chuyna.

"My payments to Mr. Sikes weren't a hardship at first. Malta grew heartily on the river banks back then. Sometimes, Tel would even help me collect it and wrap the bundle before I brought it into town.

"The sickness gradually dwindled. Those who were weak had already died, and those left were either strong enough to overcome it or immune. More people started moving into town. They brought their noisy machines and smoke, killing the river silkka for their fur and cutting down trees to build their dwellings and shops. Soon the mountain began to look very different. Even the river shrank back as if weary of the encroachment of men.

"Malta became scarce, and even when I could find it, the leaves were withered and limp. Mr. Sikes sometimes frowned at what I brought, but he never said anything. Soon it took me and Tel a whole week of scavenging to find enough to fill a bundle. Our family suffered. The younger ones tried to pitch in more, but it wasn't enough. They needed my experience to help them with the planting and hunting, but I was always after malta to pay back Mr. Sikes.

"Finally, it got to the point where there simply wasn't any malta left. I brought him a handful of leaves, the last that anyone in my family could find on our side of Dun Mountain. We had scoured high and low. This was truly the last.

"For a while, Mr. Sikes was silent. He just stood there, facing me, shaking his head.

"'I'm sorry, child. I've almost grown to like you over the years. Even been covering for you lately when you've brought me lower-quality malta. But if what you say is true, and this is the last of it, this is where our agreement comes to its end. It's funny, but I really was rooting for you to pay it all off. And you were close, closer than anyone else I've ever had.'

"I was a little older then. I didn't cry or beg. I just met his gaze and said, 'I have no regrets. Tel is alive because of our agreement. So what happens now, Mr. Sikes?'

"He looked away first. 'I'll have to send for the reckoners. They'll come to collect you.'

"I had heard stories of the reckoners as a child. Villagers used to say they were demons that crept into town at night and carried people into the valley to eat them alive. As I grew older, I began to believe these were just tales shared to keep children in line. Now, I would have to face them in person.

"'Where will they take me? For how long?'

"'They'll take you to Gehenna until you work off your debt.'

"I relaxed slightly. 'But you said there's not much left. If I work there and Tel works here, I'm sure we'll pay it off soon. Maybe I'll even return by winter.'

"It was spring then, I remember, because the Chiksa were in bloom as I walked home from town.

"'Maybe you will, child.' But Mr. Sikes couldn't meet my gaze as he said it.

"The wagon came for me the next day, and I stepped into it willingly after Tel gave me once last fierce hug.

"'I'll help you, Sister,' he whispered before releasing me. 'We'll see you return before Dun has its first snow.'

"I gripped his hand tightly as I stepped into the wagon. 'I have no regrets,' I told him, love overflowing from my heart to see him healthy and strong, already a young man.

"The doors closed, and I was caged in. It made me sympathetic for all the animals caught in Tel's traps, what they must have felt. I waved at Tel through the bars, and he chased after the wagon for a while, shouting promises to me.

"It was the last time I saw him."

# CHAPTER 14

Agatha swallowed and wrapped her bony arms around herself. She drew her gaze up from the ground. The muscles in her neck were taunt like corded ropes straining against a heavy load.

"Lucien has kept me here my whole life, working to pay off my debt."

"Lucien," Arnion said quietly. His grip on the rock ledge tightened for a moment. "He is the ultimate deceiver, burdening you with debts you could never hope to be released from."

By this time, Has and Eril had finished dispensing water and made their way toward Arnion. The group of people was large, and yet it was quiet as if a hush had fallen over everyone at once. Has shuffled his feet in the dust for a moment and then spoke.

"Arnion, ye've freely given of yerself and taught us how to draw water from the rock. And ye've reminded this old codger what it's like to be a person again. In the midst of Gehenna, I'd say that's the even greater feat. I don't know why ye chose to come here, but I'm glad ye did. If anyone else talked of freeing us from Lucien, I'd think they were daft, but with ye, my old heart dares to hope."

Has met Arnion's eyes, and his dusty face split into a grin. The two man clasped their forearms in a solid grip for a moment before letting go.

"Thank you for the vote of confidence, Has. I will find a way to free you. I swear it."

There was a collective sigh as if all the people gathered released their breath at once. Some smiled. Others laughed and shook hands. Arnion dismissed the assembly, and the crowd began to disperse, each headed back to his or her workstation. Acadia bent down in a stretch and touched her toes briefly, yawning.

Arnion chuckled. "Did we tire you out today?"

"No, I just feel so relaxed. I can't explain it."

Acadia finished her stretch and turned to face him. He took her hand in his as they made their way back over the ridge and circled around the mounds of gravel close to their worksite.

"I used to think you were a little daft myself."

"Really?" Arnion met her playful expression with raised eyebrows. "What changed?"

"I'm not sure exactly. Nothing I can put into words, anyway."

Acadia could feel herself beginning to blush. She fiddled with her fingers for a moment before turning her gaze to study the ground in front of them.

*What did change my mind?*

Arnion opened his mouth to reply, but before he could get the words out, the ground was rocked by an immense explosion. Acadia thought she might be sick as the rocks beneath her roiled and churned like waves on the sea. She clung to Arnion like a life raft. His footing was impossibly steady, and he held her tight until the ground stopped shaking.

A dense black cloud of smoke was billowing up from one of the quarry sites further away. Acadia couldn't see its source. Dust fell around them like snow, mingled with flecks of black ash.

"Are you all right?" Arnion cupped Acadia's cheek, and his eyes scanned her over, checking for injuries.

"Y-yes, I'm fine," Acadia stammered. "What just happened?"

Arnion released her and fixed his gaze on the black cloud forming out of the rising smoke in the distance. "I'm not sure. An explosion of some kind."

The guards had stumbled out of their shack, torn from their naps by the abrupt blast that rocked the quarry. Angrily, they began shouting out questions at the prisoners.

"Why have you all stopped working?"

"What happened?"

"What's all that smoke over there?"

One of the guards grabbed a prisoner by his neck and shook him, trying to get answers, but the man was speechless. No one knew what had happened. Disgusted, the guard threw him to the ground. More guards began pouring out of the compound. Whips cracked. Bludgeon sticks thudded against flesh.

"All right, you swine get back to work."

Anyone who lingered too long staring at the black cloud in the distance was soon inflicted with a smarting new bruise.

"Nothing to see here. Lucien has it all under control."

The guards were unanimous in their orders and merciless with their discipline. Soon, all the prisoners were back at their posts, working as if nothing had happened.

Arnion surreptitiously kept his eyes on what was unfolding in the distance. Wagons had begun exiting the compound and heading toward the site of the explosion.

*Lucien must be there,* Arnion realized. *He's been looking for something all this time, and now, he's finally found it.*

Arnion reached into his spirit and sent out a furtive probe. Whatever had set off that explosion was powerful. His spirit naturally recoiled from it, without knowing what it was. He felt it shrink back as if frightened.

*What has Lucien uncovered out there?*

Arnion was concerned by the reticence in his spirit. As he retracted it, he was left with a lingering sense of darkness. It left an acrid taste in his mouth and set his teeth on edge.

Throughout the day, thoughts about the explosion and what it could mean kept roving around Arnion's mind. As he chipped at the kelsum walls in front of him, his resolve was hardening like iron. He needed to find out what was discovered today. Something had just been set in motion, and he knew it was nearly time to free the people of Gehenna from Lucien's unbreakable grip.

Since coming here, he had heard story after story of how people got themselves into debt. Agatha's account today was just one of thousands like it. Foolish people, unlucky people, and even generous people like Agatha sold their freedom to obtain things from the Heartless King. But once they got here, Lucien made sure that they would never be able to leave.

Eiren's analysts insisted that all signs pointed toward an imminent military action; Gehenna was preparing for war.

*From what I can see, these people are beaten down and dying. It doesn't seem likely that they could take up arms against anyone.*

With each blow of his pickaxe, chunks of kelsum came loose from the wall. Arnion could feel his muscles tense under his skin. He was so deep in thought that he didn't realize how hard he had been pushing himself. Sweat was dripping off his eyebrows and chin. He paused for a moment to swipe at it with the corner of his shirt.

*If Rhys could see me now…* The corner of his mouth pulled up in a small smile. *Well, I'll be seeing him again soon enough.*

The workforce was finally released for the night. People hurried to go throw themselves on the floors of their cells in the compound for a few brief hours of restless sleep before their torment in the quarry would start over again. Arnion turned to slip away from the trudging mass when he found Acadia blocking his path.

"Where are you going?" Her feet were planted firmly apart, and her arms were crossed.

"Acadia, you should head back. There's something I need to do."

"You're going to check out that explosion from earlier today, aren't you?"

Arnion frowned. He had forgotten how perceptive she could be. "I'll be fine." He placed his hands on her shoulders and steered her toward the compound. "But it could be dangerous for you. I don't want you getting hurt. Go back. I'll tell you what I find out tomorrow."

She turned in his arms till she was facing him, biting her bottom lip. Her hands drifted up to settle on his chest and she could feel his heartbeat beneath her palm.

"Acadia," Arnion spoke softly, hands sliding down from her shoulders to her forearms.

Clutching the fabric of his shirt, she looked up suddenly, startling him. "Don't send me away, Arnion. Please," she pleaded.

Arnion covered her hands with his and tried to pry his shirt from her grasp, but she held fast.

"Don't tell me to go back." Her voice was quiet but decided.

He lifted his right hand and gently cradled her face.

"Acadia," he spoke firmly, but she could sense he was weakening.

Acadia mimicked his gesture and put her right hand to his cheek. "Where you go, I will go."

Her expression was fierce. Arnion could sense the determination rolling off her like electricity from a storm cloud.

"All right," he whispered.

His breath ghosted across her lips, and Acadia shivered. Slowly, she lowered her arm. Trying to muster up some bravado, she tossed her head back.

"Good." She tried to project a tone of confident assurance but wasn't quite sure she succeeded. Acadia cleared her throat. "So what's the plan?"

# CHAPTER 15

The hand that had been holding her face so tenderly dropped back to Arnion's side. Acadia missed the warmth of his calloused palm against her cheek. She picked at the smoke rash between her knuckles to distract herself from the thought.

Arnion covered her hand with his, preventing her from scratching further.

"I don't know if I'd really go so far to call it a plan, but I need to find out what Lucien's up to. I intend to get as close to the site of the blast as possible and see what I can find out. Maybe there won't be anything left. Lucien could have covered his tracks already."

The murky gray sky was slowly fading to black above them. The wind howled through the quarry, stirring up fragments of rock and dust in tiny dervishes. Acadia nudged at a hunk of kelsum with her foot.

"And what if Lucien has moved it already?"

Arnion's visage steeled for a moment. "Then it might be a long night." The intensity in his eyes melted away as quickly as it had appeared. His eyes crinkled up into his trademark grin. "But let's not worry about that till we come to it."

The hand that was covering Acadia's entwined its fingers through hers. He tugged her gently. "Shall we get started?"

Acadia squeezed his hand.

"Okay."

She matched her pace with his limping stride subconsciously. They didn't rush. There was no need. The quarry was completely deserted. The guards had all gone back into the compound, celebrating another hard day of cruelty around spits of glistening roast meat and bottles of thick red wine. Soon they would begin to fall asleep in piles around the fire, much warmer and more comfortable than the prisoners shivering in their drafty cells.

Despite the raging wind around her, Acadia felt as if their every footstep echoed through the canyon, a screaming beacon alerting anyone nearby of their location. She kept snatching furtive glances over her shoulder. At any moment, Acadia expected to see the guards swarming out of the compound, heading straight for them.

While her gaze scanned the distant lights of the compound once more, Arnion nudged her shoulder mischievously. "Why are you so worried, Acadia?"

She flinched at being caught.

*So much for subtlety*, she thought wryly. "I'm not worried."

He raised an eyebrow at her.

"Okay, maybe I'm a little concerned, seeing as how every tread of our feet sounds like a herd of elephants bellowing through a canyon."

"Even with all this wind." He gestured to the dust churning around them.

Acadia huffed. "It's still not impossible that someone might notice us out here."

"You're right," he conceded. "But that's why I'm shielding us with my spirit. Unless another person who's highly competent in spirit use crosses our path, we should be safe."

"You can do that?"

"Our spirits are capable of much more than those of you in Gehenna have realized."

Acadia looked at him curiously. "Do you think I could sense your shielding?"

"If you know how to look for it. Do you remember what I taught you?"

"Yes, I think so. Let me try."

Despite the gale around her, Acadia sought to quiet her mind. Her worries were quickly forgotten with the certainty that Arnion was protecting her, and she was tremendously eager to try any spirit exercise he gave her. Acadia reached in toward her spirit. It was like a hesitant blue candle flame within her center. She coaxed it a little brighter and felt a tremble like electricity pass through her arms.

*Okay, spirit,* Acadia thought, *let's look for Arnion's shield.*

Holding it tightly within her, she fixed her sight on Arnion. So far, she didn't notice anything different. He had let go of her hand and was waiting expectantly. Acadia exhaled and tried again.

*Okay, spirit, let's try once more. Arnion is projecting a shield.*

She pictured a large metal shield like the knights in her childhood storybooks used to carry.

*A shield around us to protect us. Help me find it.*

She could feel her spirit burning brightly now. Its force flowed through her, a powerful and yet gentle presence. Acadia returned her concentration to her physical sight and was amazed to see a translucent golden sphere materialize around Arnion and herself. The shield shimmered around them, sparking with the air. The dust quivered by their feet where its force met with the ground.

"Arnion, I can see it," she gasped. "The shield, it's beautiful. It looks like a giant golden bubble protecting us from the dust."

"Well done, Acadia!"

He grasped both her hands in an impulse of pleasure. She abruptly lost her concentration, and the vision faded away.

"I'm impressed by how quickly you're learning."

She looked down, embarrassed. "All this time we've been walking, you've been protecting me, and I didn't even notice."

The gale seethed around them, and yet within the sphere, not a flake of dust stirred that wasn't kicked up by their own feet.

"You're amazing, Arnion."

It was the prince's turn to blush. "It's no trouble, Acadia. It makes me happy to protect you." He met her gaze, eyes serious.

Somehow, they had stopped walking. Arnion was still looking at her with an intensity that pulled her in. An emotion swam in the depths of his expression, something unnamed, and it made Acadia's pulse quicken in her throat. She found she couldn't look away, couldn't bear to break the eye contact and the fragile hopes that were forming inside her like a delicate crystalline structure. Acadia reached up—to do what exactly she wasn't sure. But she couldn't stop herself from reaching toward him. She wanted to capture this moment and hold onto it forever to extract the meaning out that exquisite look in his eyes.

Unfortunately, her action had the opposite of its intended effect. As her hand moved toward his face, Arnion blinked and seemed to snap out of the spell he was under. He took her hand and brought it to his cheek, pressing a tender kiss against the inside of her palm.

"I'm sorry, Acadia. I lost myself for a moment there."

She spluttered out something incoherent, and he smiled. By now, she had gotten used to the contorted grimace that passed for a smile in Arnion's marred face. More often than not, she found its appearance now tugged a grin from her own lips as well. So she made an effort to clamp down her disappointment and return Arnion's cheerful expression, but her heart ached to explore that unspoken emotion more fully.

A sudden realization flashed across her mind. She thumped Arnion playfully on the arm.

"So that's how you've been keeping the guards from noticing us all this time."

With an embarrassed shrug, he replied, "Well, more or less."

Arnion was on the verge of speaking again when he stopped short and held up a hand protectively in front of her. Acadia was caught off guard and bumped into him. At his expression, she swallowed her questions down and waited for him to explain.

"We're getting close."

Arnion spoke quietly, and Acadia wanted to slap herself. She had completely forgotten why they had come. They were here to investigate Lucien and whatever abominable scheme he was planning.

*And here I am getting completely distracted by Arnion. Now is definitely not the time for this.*

She gave herself a mental shake to drive the point home. The gusts of wind began to carry along wisps of a pungent odor. At first, it was intermittent but grew stronger as they approached the site of the blast. Black scorch marks began to appear, blistered along the kelsum walls. Arnion's countenance took on a pale gravity that Acadia had never seen before. They were treading on ash now. A layer of it covered the ground around them like a dirty snowfall. The stench became so vile that her nose wrinkled involuntarily, and she soon had to pinch it shut with her hand to prevent herself from gagging.

There before them lay a jagged hole in the quarry wall. Patches of smoke still smoldered around its edges. This was definitely the source of the fetid smell. It swam through the air like a malevolent creature encircling them in its tentacles. The gaping maw of the explosion seemed to suck all the warmth from Acadia's body. Deep in her gut, an instinctive desire to flee from this place rose up unbidden.

She clenched Arnion's hand and managed to squeak out, "What is this?"

Arnion had extended his free hand toward the sinister darkness before them. At her words, he tore his gaze away from it and looked at her, unseeing for a moment. She tugged at him desperately and repeated her question.

"Arnion, what is this? This place terrifies me!"

His focus returned to her face, but she could tell his attention was divided.

"This is Eiren's greatest fear. Lucien has discovered a vein of trividium."

Acadia had never seen him look so unsettled. Throughout all the horrors of Gehenna, Arnion had projected a quiet confidence and peace that drew others to himself like a healing balm. Even his anguish during the weekly spectacles was nothing compared to this.

"What do you mean Eiren's greatest fear? Eiren is the greatest civilization on the planet. What could they possibly have to be afraid of?"

A gust of air tugged at her shirt, adding to the chill she already felt. Grit brushed against her face, and Acadia tried to turn her face away from the wind.

*Wait, the wind? Why can I feel it all of a sudden?* "Arnion, what's happening to your shield?" Her voice wavered.

"It's weakening," he told her grimly. "I'm sorry, Acadia. I never should have brought you here. I was so desperate to believe that my hunch was wrong, and now I've exposed you to great danger."

His voice was hoarse, his distress palpable. Acadia's heart wrenched in her chest at the wretched expression in his eyes.

Another blast of air ripped between them, and Acadia realized that they were caught with a formidable sandstorm between them and the compound.

"How much longer can your shield hold out?"

"Not long."

She noticed that they both now had to strain their voices to be heard over the gale.

"I will keep it up as long as I can, but it will eventually fail. We need to find some kind of shelter."

"And get away from that horrible thing." She pointed back toward the charred scar behind them. Arnion nodded, grasping her hand in a sweat-slicked palm.

They trundled against the relentless wind. No matter which direction they turned, it seemed to be against them. After a few minutes, Arnion stumbled and fell.

Dropping to her knees beside him, Acadia placed her hand on his forehead. "Arnion, are you all right? You're burning up."

He met her gaze, and she was relieved to see some of the usual buoyancy had returned to his eyes.

"I'm all right, Acadia. Just a little tired."

She helped him to his feet. After he stumbled a second time, she wrapped an arm around his waist to support him. Arnion tried to protest, but at the dogged expression on her face, he conceded. He ran his fingers over the prickly stubble at the back of her head and settled his arm about her neck with a weary thanks.

On and on, they walked, each step draining their strength. Sweat was soaking through Arnion's shirt now. Acadia could feel the wetness seeping through her hold on his back. She blinked back tears from her eyes brought on by both the sand and a feeling of hopelessness.

"Acadia, look over there. Do you see it?"

Arnion's neck was strained toward a shadowy lump about fifty feet away. Acadia squinted her eyes in that direction.

"It looks like a cluster of rocks."

"That might work," Arnion wheezed. He fought the urge to sag against her in exhaustion. "Let's go."

Rallying the last of his strength, Arnion tugged Acadia toward the outcropping. As they got closer, he squeezed her hand before releasing it. "Look for an opening. We need to get out of this wind," he rasped.

The boulders were cool to the touch as they each groped around the stones, searching.

"Arnion, I've found something!" Acadia shouted, desperately hoping he could hear her over the wind.

After a few breathless moments, he appeared beside her. The rocks leaned against each other at an angle, forming a small triangular opening that they could both crawl into. Inside was cramped, and the musty smell of ancient stone filled the air, but it was free from the worst of the wind. Arnion let out a ragged breath, and Acadia could sense the shield collapse entirely.

# CHAPTER 16

It was dark within the crevice. Outside, the wind still howled and spewed sand about like a kryet in heat. The noise from the storm made talking impossible. Arnion lay with his back against the opening, sealing it off as much as he was able. Acadia nestled up against him, her back pressed into his chest. He wrapped an arm around her, pulling her close. Arnion took her hand and guided it to his face. Acadia could feel that he had pulled the edge of his shirt up to protect his nose and mouth.

*Ah, he's telling me I should do the same*, she realized.

Despite the utter blackness, Acadia felt calm. She could feel Arnion's chest rising and falling with his breath. He was warm, and the weight of his arm holding her gave her an inexplicable sense of assurance, not at all like the feeling she got staring at the remains of the hole ripped into the quarry wall earlier today. Acadia shuddered at the memory.

<Are you cold?>

She felt rather than heard Arnion's voice.

*It's his spirit*, Acadia realized. *He's using it to communicate to me without speaking.*

She quieted her mind and sent a hesitant tendril back. <Arnion? I'm all right. Can you hear me?>

His arm squeezed her gently, and she felt his reply. <Yes!>

<What is this?> She asked internally. <How can I hear you in my head?>

She could feel his chuckle bubbling through his response. There was something else mixed in there too, but Acadia couldn't quite put her finger on it.

<We are speaking directly through our spirits to one another. Where I come from, long-distance communication like this is quite common. We call it spir-com. The more you practice, the farther you will be able to project.>

It was uncanny, hearing his voice inside her mind. A few months ago, she would have thought she was mad, hearing voices in her head. But it was Arnion, without a doubt. She could feel his presence within her spirit as surely as she could feel his body pressed against her.

Acadia wanted to turn around and soak in the pleased expression she knew was coloring his face. But it was cramped and dark, plus she had to keep her eyelids scrunched up tight to protect them from the sand. Arnion was probably doing the same, she suspected. So instead, Acadia settled for hugging the arm that was wrapped around her, pulling it close.

A burst of color filled her mind, rosy pink fading to red with swirls of gold curling out the edges. She gasped out loud and coughed as sand swirled into her mouth. After a moment to regain her breath, she tried again.

<Arnion, was that you?>

<Yes. I'm sorry, I forgot for a moment. You sent a syna to me just now, and I responded to it without thinking.>

<I sent a what?>

She felt another chuckle coming through him, both in her spirit and rumbling off his chest.

<A syna. It looked something like this.>

Again, Acadia's spirit was filled with a barrage of colors. Giant glittering bubbles of emerald-green and orangey citrine floated up. They jostled one another cheerfully and popped in sloppy iridescent splashes behind her eyes.

<We use synas to send emotions we can't always put into words.>

<And I sent one to you without realizing it?>

Acadia felt mortified. It was one thing to willingly communicate thoughts but a different thing entirely to unwittingly send Arnion her emotions on a silver platter.

As if sensing her embarrassment, she felt him reassure her.

<It's a good thing, Acadia. It means your spirit is getting stronger. You just have to keep in mind that talking through one's spirit can be a little more transparent than traditional speech.>

She felt a soothing ripple of blue waves pass through her.

<They are beautiful.> She conceded.

Acadia attempted to mold her emotions into a conscious syna to send to Arnion. She felt a twirling vortex of green and yellow slashes leave her spirit.

*I might be able to get the hang of this*, she thought.

The swirl of colors twisted away out of sight, and Acadia suddenly remembered.

<Arnion, back there at that terrible place, you spoke of Eiren?>

Acadia made a conscious effort not to project her fears through her spirit. Still, she could sense an image of curling gray smoke rising in her as an afterthought.

<Yes.> His voice was firm and resolved, even in her mind. <Acadia, do you remember when we first met?>

Yes, she did. Even in the dark, her face burned with shame at the memory. He had distracted the guards and protected her from a vicious assault. In return, she had spoken harshly to him and even laughed in his face. She had apologized more than once since then, but the thought of her actions still made her cringe. Acadia never realized she had been capable of such cruelty until she entered Gehenna.

Arnion was another story. It always struck her how he never held her prior behavior over her head, like a hammer waiting to fall. He accepted her apologies gently and assured her the matter was finished. Even before she had apologized, even while she was still being dismissive and rude, Arnion had always been kind and respectful to her.

<You really are from Eiren, aren't you?>

His affirmation confirmed what she already knew deep down, the thoughts she had been deliberately avoiding for some time. Acadia didn't know whether she wanted to laugh or cry. A part of her desperately wanted to crawl out from their shelter and scream into the wind until she had no voice left. Lucien's cruelty was already legendary, but his treatment of Elyon's ambassadors bordered on fanatical. Arnion knew this, and still he had come.

<I told you on that day why I was here. Do you remember?>

She did.

<To rescue us.>

Her heart pounded within her chest. *Could he really do it? Was there a chance that we could actually escape Gehenna?* Acadia swallowed, crushing down her hope into a tiny pinprick that she pushed to the back of her mind.

Arnion's spirit whispered urgently to her. <Now that Lucien has discovered trividium here, it is even more crucial that we evacuate everyone as soon as possible.>

She could hear the strain in his voice as clearly as if he was actually speaking. Even in this moment, he was worried for them rather than himself.

<Arnion, what is trividium? Why does Eiren fear it?>

Arnion sighed, and she could feel it against the back of her neck.

<It's not the trividium in itself, though it is a foul, loathsome substance. They fear what Lucien will do when he gets his hands on it. The loss of life from his experiments last time was catastrophic. They fear what it will cost to stop him a second time.>

<You mean Lucien has fought with Eiren before?>

It made sense now that Acadia thought about it. Lucien was obsessed with Eiren. His hatred for Elyon and his ambassadors had to stem from somewhere.

<Lucien is from Eiren. He was one of its chief citizens, viceroy to the king. Lucien used to govern the entire kingdom, second only to Elyon himself.>

Acadia could swear she felt the world suddenly shift. It felt like everything she knew was falling out from under her. She clutched at Arnion desperately and tried to keep her emotions under control as she replied. <Wait, you're telling me Lucien is from Eiren? The Heartless King who snatches people away and forces them to work as prisoners, brutalized every day in his kelsum quarries?>

<Regrettably, yes.>

Arnion's spirit was grieved. She could feel it seeping into his responses.

<But I thought Eiren was supposed to be this wonderful place. Everyone always describes it like a paradise, filled with beauty and wealth beyond imagining.> Acadia couldn't contain her questions, they spilled from her mind in a rush.

His spirit was reassuring, though pain still swam beneath the surface. <Eiren is an incredible place, Acadia, and it was during Lucien's time as well. Lucien was more than just a viceroy to the king. He and my father were as close as brothers. But when trividium was discovered in Eiren, Lucien changed. He saw the raw power it could unleash, and he became utterly consumed by it. Elyon forbid him to continue experimenting, and so Lucien plotted to overthrow his rule, taking a third of the royal guard with him. In my country, we call this the Fall, when the Deceiver instigated a civil war and the nation was divided.>

Arnion let his sadness wash over him for a moment, regret for all the pain and suffering that had ripped his kingdom wide open. Even though it was before his time, he felt the grief of his people. Anger coursed through him as well.

<Lucien didn't stop at betraying his people and dividing his homeland. He thrives on oppressing the weak. It's clear to me now that he'll never be satisfied with Eiren or Gehenna, he won't be content until he's ravaged all of Elorah.>

<What happened in Eiren?>

Acadia's question shook Arnion from his ruminations.

<Lucien was defeated, but at a great cost. Brother fought against brother. Sister against sister. Father against son. Families were torn apart, and friendships broken. Those who hungered for power joined Lucien, while those loyal to the king opposed him. It was a brutal, devastating war on both sides until finally the Deceiver and his followers were expelled, exiled from Eiren forever.>

Acadia's thoughts were flooded by a powerful syna. It looked like rain cascading down onto a gray lifeless expanse. Slashes of silver blades flashed through the downpour. A dark red seeped up from the ground, swallowing the surface. Rain pelted down into rippling crimson puddles. The image faded away to black.

She swallowed, trying to get rid of the dry feeling in her throat. <That's why he hates Eiren so much.>

Arnion's embrace of Acadia loosened as he became absorbed in his thoughts.

<When Lucien was exiled, he vowed that one day he would have his revenge. We thought the suffering he inflicted on innocents in Gehenna was enough torment for my father. There were always rumors, of course, but I was never fully convinced that he would attempt to assault Eiren again, until now.>

<Arnion, what does trividium do?>

For a moment, Arnion's spirit was silent. She could feel him hesitating. Finally, she felt his voice once more.

<It kills a person's spirit. Outwardly, they are alive, filled with great power. But the people they were before are dead. You can see it in their eyes. A dark murderous hunger fills them. They don't stop even if their bodies are being torn apart. They will still try to inflict suffering and mayhem on all who oppose them until their last breath.>

Arnion's body shuddered, and he buried his face in the space between her neck and her collarbone.

<It's a horrible thing to witness, Acadia, the way a person is lost to trividium.>

In an unconscious gesture of comfort, she turned and drew her arms around his neck, nestling her head under his chin. <Will something happen to us?> She tightened her embrace, cinching her hands in the collar of his shirt. <We were right at the site where Lucien found it.>

Arnion rubbed her back in soothing circles.

<Other than a temporary weakening of our spirit abilities, no. Lucien's experiments involved finding ways to incorporate trividium within the human system. He would inject his subjects with various compounds meant to heighten the effects, trying to find the right dosage to maximize their power while still being able to control them.>

An image of figures drenched in red sludge filled her mind. Their mouths opened in voiceless screams, tearing at the crimson filth that enveloped them. In agony, their shapes twisted and dissolved into nothing. Acadia shuddered. Syna were not just used to convey pleasant emotions, apparently.

<That's horrific. Those poor people.>

<It was. Lucien unleashed them on the unsuspecting towns of Eiren. His warriors didn't just slaughter soldiers. Children, the elderly, the weak and infirm, all fell under their blades. The only consolation was that trividium had to be taken willingly.>

<What do you mean?>

<If Lucien tried to force trividium into someone, their spirit can reject it. Body and spirit rage in conflict with each other, and within days, the person would waste away and die. It is an agonizing death. Those of his test subjects who were discovered mid-experiment begged to be destroyed to end their suffering. Only those who truly desire to cling to trividium's dark power can be transformed by it. They exchange the life-giving power of their spirit for its caliginous strength.>

The thoughts that accompanied his words made Acadia shiver. She was just learning how to use her spirit. It had seemed like such a great reservoir of invincible strength.

*At least, Arnion made it seem that way.*

She had always assumed his confidence flowed from being able to rely on its incredible power. But now, there was something that could devour a person's spirit. She could feel the small seed of hope crack a little within her breast.

Tentatively she asked, <Can its effects be reversed?>

His voice was weighed down with sadness in her mind. <We have never seen it happen. To be consumed by trividium is to willingly give the most precious part of yourself over to a sinister darkness in a quest for power. Once you make that choice, I'm not sure there is a way to go back.>

Acadia regretted asking. The topic clearly pained Arnion. *Who could blame him? It all sounds terrifying.*

She wanted to think of something comforting to say, but her mind was drawing a complete blank. The circumstances Arnion described were so frightening that she could hardly wrap her head around them.

It was clear that his nation's past was still a grievous wound to him.

*Sometimes, there's nothing anyone can say to make things better,* she thought to herself.

So instead, she sought to comfort him with her presence. Curled up against him, she remained quiet as the memory of Eiren's suffering washed over him for a time.

Acadia had no idea how long they lay there together. It could have been minutes or hours. There was no way for her to tell at the moment. But somewhere during the course of the night, the storm began to die down. The wind still whispered around the rocks outside, but it appeared the majority of its fury was spent. She pulled the edge of her shirt away from her nose and mouth. The sand that was caked on it crumbled under her hands.

Brushing it off her eyebrows, Acadia tried to delicately extract it from her lashes. Running a hand over her scalp, she curled her toes at the unpleasant sensation of all the grains stuck in her cropped hair. She couldn't even imagine what she must look like. Thankfully, it was still dark in the crevice they sheltered in.

# CHAPTER 17

Arnion felt her shifting and guessed at what she was doing.

"The storm seems to be letting up," he whispered. His voice was hoarse and dry. They had shelter for the moment, but they would need food soon to keep up their strength. He shook the sand from his shirt, keeping his eyes shut tight.

The ground underneath them had been cool at first, but now, it was warm from their body heat. Acadia was warm too, still snuggled against his chest. She was thin and wiry in his arms but not frail. Despite the daily struggle to survive in Gehenna, she retained an inner strength. Arnion ran a hand along her forearm up to her shoulder and back down again.

"Thank you for coming with me, Acadia. I appreciate your kindness. Many times, I've wondered how someone like you could ever wind up here." He spoke quietly. Immediately, he could feel her tense up and regretted that he had voiced his thoughts even if it had been an ever-increasing question in his mind.

"Never mind, you don't have to answer that, Acadia," he said, drawing her closer. "Whatever your past was, it's over. It's who you are today that matters."

He could feel her breath against his neck, soft puffs of warm air that tickled slightly. Arnion steeled himself not to squirm, waiting. Since his ill-timed question, Acadia had gone rigid in his arms, not speaking a word. Arnion was patient, and he allowed the silence to stretch on between them.

When he began to feel the light patter of tears dripping from her face and pooling in the hollow of his throat, he could bear it no longer. "Acadia, what you've done before isn't going to change anything between us, you know that right?"

She was the one crying, and yet he found himself undone. Desperate to give her comfort, he began stroking her face, planting soft kisses on her forehead and cheekbones. Soon, he found himself kissing away the tears as they fell.

She took a shuddering breath and said in a quavering voice, "Oh, Arnion, you don't know the things I've done. If you really knew me, you would be appalled. I deserve to be here. I don't deserve a second chance."

Acadia fisted her hands in his shirt and began to cry harder. Arnion took her chin gently in his hand and lifted her face to his.

"You let me be the judge of that."

He kissed her, and she clung to him like a lifeline. Acadia didn't even register when her tears stopped and dried in salty tracks down her face. She was overwhelmed by Arnion's gentleness and his kindness to her. His tender kisses lit a fire in her belly, and she returned them hungrily. Acadia had never met anyone like Arnion before. She knew she was in love with him. Citizen of Eiren or not, it didn't matter. If he said that her past didn't matter to him, she desperately wanted to take him at his word.

*Even if I get what I deserve and remain a prisoner in Gehenna for the rest of my life, Lucien will never be able to take away the memory of this feeling that burns through my veins. He will never be able to quench my love for Arnion.*

In that moment, Acadia decided that she wanted to tell Arnion everything. She would tell him about her past, her deal with Lucien, and how she ended up in Gehenna. It was a story she had never shared with another living soul. Deep down, Acadia had already condemned herself, knowing that Gehenna was where she belonged, but that didn't mean she wanted to hear it confirmed by others. Arnion deserved the truth though. He was a light that had shown into the blackest darkness she had known. Acadia wanted to tell him everything. It would be a relief, finally putting aside burdens she had secretly carried all this time.

*Is it possible that he could still care for me, knowing all that I've done?*

Acadia wasn't sure. Her mind told her it was impossible, but her heart pumped courage into her.

*At the very least, I won't have to live with the fear that he might discover the truth about my past some other way.*

They broke apart, and Acadia pressed her forehead against his, heart pounding.

Arnion nuzzled his nose against hers and whispered, "Wow."

A chuckle rose unbidden from Acadia's lips. "Wow," she repeated, smiling.

Arnion lightly traced his fingers along her jawline. His voice was awestruck. "I never expected this to happen, Acadia. From the first minute I saw you, I've wanted to know you. You've captivated me completely."

She drew his hand down from her face and clasped it between hers. "I've never told anyone how I ended up here, Arnion. I'm ashamed of what I've done."

Arnion squeezed her hands but didn't say anything. He didn't want to push her or make her feel trapped. As a young child, he loved watching insects. One of the easiest to spot were the jadette butterflies that frequented the garden. Their graceful beauty and brilliant colors fascinated him. At first, he chased after them waving his arms, pleading with them to land. His father, noticing his crestfallen face later that day, suggested that he try standing perfectly still. Although Arnion was skeptical at first, he was delighted when the advice proved true. The next day after waiting with bated breath, a radiant green and purple jadette landed on his shoulder. Acadia was worth more than a thousand butterflies, and Arnion would have sat still for days, if necessary, to make her feel safe.

Acadia was grateful for his patience. A couple of times, she opened her mouth to speak but didn't have the courage to push the words from her throat. She went to scratch at her knuckles but found Arnion's hand blocking her.

"Please don't, chimad," he told her with quiet reproach.

Acadia wanted to roll her eyes at him, but it was still a little too dark for her gesture to be appreciated. So she settled for huffing her breath loudly and pulling her hands free.

"Chimad?" she repeated.

"It's a secret."

She could practically hear him winking at her.

"Arnion," she said in a warning tone and pinched his shoulder.

"Ouch!" He rubbed where she had pinched him. "I'll tell you sometime, I promise. Once when we've left Gehenna."

Acadia's breath caught in her throat.

*Leave Gehenna?*

She could barely even entertain the hope of such a thought. It was like a tiny balloon floating over a sea of needles. The reality she had known for so long wanted to crush it mercilessly.

*If I could just start over, together with Arnion, then anything was possible. I could be content to live in a hovel in the southern wastelands,* she thought to herself. The concept surprised her, but she recognized it as the truth.

"I grew up in a small farming village about a half day's journey from Beulah," she blurted out before she could lose her nerve.

Feeling Arnion nod in encouragement, Acadia was thankful that it was too dark for her to be able to see him clearly. She didn't want to see his face when she told him.

Picking at an uneven spot on her thumbnail, she forced herself to continue, "My parents have a small farm out there. Mostly fruit trees, vegetable plots, and a couple sagrin that we were able to purchase after scrapping together our savings for a few years."

Her heart was pounding so hard that she felt it might burst. There was a creeping ache crawling from the pit of her stomach up her spine.

*I've tried not to think about them for so long,* she realized.

When her pause stretched on for a few moments, Arnion rubbed her arm, encouragingly.

"I'm sorry," she said, voice brittle. "I just haven't spoken of them for so long. I tried so hard to pretend I'd forgotten them." Her voice broke. "I don't know if they could ever forgive me."

The last sentence was a whisper laced with pain.

"Then Da got sick. He had a bad fall, injured his head. He couldn't work."

The words were gushing out of her now, an uncontrollable torrent like floodwaters bursting through a dam.

"We all tried to pitch in extra to make up for it, my ma, my two younger brothers, and myself. But it wasn't working. Ma decided we would need to sell the sagrins for food. She sent me into town, begged me to get a good price for them. We'd need it to survive until Da was well again."

Hot tears of shame gathered at the corners of her eyes. Acadia was glad that Arnion couldn't see her face turn its usual blotchy red when she got emotional. She swallowed and forced herself to continue.

"I used to get so jealous of the women there with their elegant flowing robes. Once, a woman's scarf was tossed up in the air by the wind. I caught it, and when I returned it to her, I noticed how soft and white her hands were. She was so beautiful without a care in the world. How could a mangy farmer's daughter with dirt under her fingernails and callouses on her palms compare?

"That was when Tallo found me. He was so handsome, dressed so elegantly, like a true gentleman from the stories. He found me crying in the dust and wiped my tears away with a silk handkerchief. He called me beautiful."

Her voice stuttered.

"No one man had ever called me that before. I was overwhelmed. He seemed so kind, so generous, and when he told me he was a requisitioner for Lucien—"

At these words, Arnion's hand tightened momentarily on her arm. He took a deep breath and relaxed his grip. "I'm sorry, Acadia." His tone was somber. "Please tell me."

She squirmed in his arms for a moment, restless.

*I wish there was some way to stretch or take a walk, anything to delay this, even just a little bit,* she thought, unnerved. The only consolation was that she didn't have to see Arnion's eyes watching her intently like she knew he would be.

"I'm sure you can already tell, I bought his lies. He told me that I was beautiful, that Lucien could give me everything I wanted. That

I didn't have to waste my life and my dreams sweating away on the farm for the rest of my days.

"He told me to come back tomorrow in my best dress. But, Arnion, I had nothing, nothing other than the clothes on my back."

She dug her nails into her skin, tormented by the memory.

"I took the money from selling the sagrins, and I bought a robe and some Pali sandals from a secondhand store. I went to the bathhouse and scrubbed all the dirt off. Then I went back to Tallo and signed my life away that very day.

"I haven't seen or heard from my family since. I don't even know if they're alive."

She choked out the words.

"I hope they are in spite of everything I've done. I heard that Ma and my brothers came looking for me a few days later, but I pleaded with Tallo to send them away. I heard him cursing them and swearing that he had never heard of me. He slammed the door in their faces, and they never came back.

"I lived in Beulah after that. For a few years, it was just like Tallo promised. My life was filled with money, power, and influence. After a while, I forgot all about what I owed. I thought I was too valuable that my debt would never be called in. I thought I was special, favored by Lucien. I thought...," Acadia stammered. "I know how foolish it is now, but I thought Lucien even loved me in a way. Then the reckoners came."

A heavy silence settled over them.

*Well, now I've done it. I've destroyed my chance with the most incredible person I've ever known.*

Biting down on her lower lip, Acadia tasted blood. She felt him pull his hand back from her arm, and her heart clenched painfully in her chest. Then she felt his arms envelop her in a tender hug.

"Acadia," he breathed in her ear, "thank you for trusting me. I don't hold your past against you."

For a moment, all she could do was breathe lightly, hands at her sides.

*I didn't think anyone would ever look at me the same if they knew. I never even told Tallo where I got the money though I'm sure he must have suspected.*

She gave Arnion time for her words to sink in and for him to recoil in disgust, but he didn't let go. After a long time, she dared to raise her trembling arms, wrapping them around him and returning his embrace. He didn't flinch away from her like she half expected him to.

Instead, he pressed a kiss behind her left ear and whispered, "I'm glad I met you, Acadia."

A slight smile tugged at the corners of her lips. "You're really amazing, Arnion. You know that, right?"

Chuckling, he nuzzled his nose against hers. "As are you, Acadia."

She laughed nervously and rubbed his arm.

"There's more I need to tell you someday, but please don't ask it of me now. Just speaking of my family after all this time, it's…" She broke off for a moment and swallowed. "It's so painful. I have so many regrets. I want to make it right someday even if I can't imagine how."

"You will."

His voice was so sure. Acadia tried to absorb the strength and assurance from his words.

*It doesn't seem possible. Then again, how many times has Arnion made me eat those words?*

A sudden thought flashed through her mind, disrupting her reasoning, and she burst out, "Wait, is it true that Eirenians live forever?"

"No, not forever, but much longer than the average person from the other Elorahian countries."

"Hmm." She raised an eyebrow. "So, how long are we talking here?"

"Ah, well…" He scratched his shoulder absentmindedly. "My father just celebrated his 813th birthday."

"What?"

Acadia's thrashing around raised a cloud of dust, and they both coughed uncomfortably for a moment.

"How is that even possible?"

"Ha, the age-old question." Arnion laughed. "Do Eirenians live longer because they have knowledge of their spirits, or do they have knowledge of their spirits because they have been able to live long enough to cultivate it?"

Acadia frowned at his chicken and the egg paradox. Then suddenly, another question hit her.

"So is Lucien really three hundred years old?"

"Much older, probably." Arnion's amusement ended abruptly at this change of topic. "He's gone by many names throughout Elorah, which is why in Eiren, we refer to him as the Deceiver."

"But he doesn't look it."

"Neither do most other Eirenians. Though he's notorious for being particularly self-absorbed with his own appearance."

Acadia could tell from his words that he was grimacing.

Wanting to distract him from this obviously unpleasant topic, she tilted her head up, intending to capture his lips in another toe-crinkling kiss. A loud growl from her stomach thwarted that plan. Acadia shrank back mortified, while Arnion chuckled and patted her on the head.

"I promise that we'll share many more moments like this, but first, let's get you something to eat."

Acadia knew Arnion well enough by now to realize he had more information that she did at the moment. It was a feeling she was beginning to recognize more and more frequently as she got to know him better. As far as she could discern, they were still surrounded by boulders and sand. There was nothing edible outside of the compound. Even the few who somehow managed to escape Gehenna were often found dead of hunger and thirst less than a stadia away. But here was Arnion, speaking cheerfully about food as if they were about to pluck it from a magical tree.

"What, did you swipe some rolls back there or something?" she asked.

He held out his palm, and she recognized the familiar white sparks as his spirit flickered along his skin. It carved a series of geometric shapes through the air, giving off a faint smell of electricity as it went.

"Mana generation is an advanced survival technique in Eiren. It's required knowledge for anyone who wants to reach the highest level of spirit mastery, from warriors and ambassadors to princes in the royal line. You never know when you might spend a day in the wilderness without sustenance readily available."

As he spoke, his spirit traced and retraced an oval shape above his hand, moving faster and faster. The lines of electricity grew thicker and thicker until there were two solid bands of white light hovering above his open palm.

Arnion breathed out. The sparks of his spirit faded away, and two thick wafers plopped into his outstretched hand. Acadia, who had by now witnessed Arnion using his spirit on many occasions, still gasped in surprise.

Hesitantly, she reached out to touch the top wafer.

"Go ahead. It's all right."

He held out his hand to her. Acadia tapped it once, twice with her index finger before reaching to take hold of the strange substance. It was heavier than it looked, like a dense flat roll slightly larger than her open hand.

"It's warm," she breathed.

"Go on, try it," Arnion urged her.

Acadia hefted the disc in her hand and sniffed it skeptically. When it passed her initial evaluation, she shrugged and took a bite. She was hungry after all, and Gehenna didn't exactly cater to picky eaters. The wafer was crisp and airy in her mouth. It had a delicate flavor like honey and almonds. After a moment, the brittle texture faded to softness as it dissolved on her tongue.

"This is delicious," she mumbled, eyes wide and mouth already stuffed with a second bite. "Really! What's it called again?"

Arnion had enjoyed Acadia's analysis of the mana. After half of her wafer disappeared in a series of happy little crunches and murmurs, he took a contented bite and sighed. It felt nostalgic to be eating food from Eiren again.

Her question caught him with his mouth full. In the halls of the palace, he would have politely chewed and swallowed before answering, but out in the wilderness, he enjoyed the moment of informality.

Pushing the wad of food to the right side of his mouth, he replied, "It's called mana." Arnion finished chewing the bite he had and swallowed.

"Mana," Acadia breathed. She was already done. Any experienced citizen of Gehenna knew that the safest place to store food was in one's own stomach. She sighed contentedly. For a single wafer, that mana had been surprisingly filling. Her stomach felt completely satisfied.

"For a little disc made of air particles, it's very tasty."

"Not air particles, but I can see why you'd think so. You're thinking of how we manipulate particles of hydrozone in the kelsum to make water. Generating things by manipulating their atomic structure is a rudimentary spirit technique. Mana is generated through sheer force of the spirit alone. There's nothing that we modify to get it. That's why it's a much more advanced technique. But when you're hungry in the wilderness, it's a valuable skill."

"Hmm," Acadia hummed, licking her fingers. "Very useful. Why haven't you shown the others? Eril or Has at least?"

"It takes a high level of spirit mastery to even generate a few pieces. It often takes pupils years of study before they are ready to generate things directly from their spirit."

Acadia poked him in the chest, sensing he was skirting around something. "How long did it take you to learn?"

Arnion felt abashed. *Acadia is always so perceptive.* "It comes very natural to me. I am unique among my people for that."

"Arnion," she said in a warning tone.

He sighed. "Not long, minutes maybe, after I understood the concept. It wasn't really as if I learned it, so much as remembered knowledge that was already buried somewhere deep down."

Acadia smothered her surprise in a mask of nonchalance, another skill she'd acquired in Gehenna.

*Leave it to Arnion to be a prodigy, even among a superadvanced civilization like Eiren.* "So you're some kind of genius, huh? Is that why they chose you?"

Arnion shook his head. "No, nothing like that. In fact, the king's advisors were very reluctant to send me. I guess you could say I was a last resort. If I can't get through to the people of Gehenna, the only other option they see is war."

Her eyes widened. In all her time in Gehenna, it never occurred to her that Eiren might want to retaliate for all the atrocities inflicted on its people.

*Of course, it should have, but Gehenna has a way of making you focus entirely on your own self-preservation.*

The diplomatic implications of the treatment of ambassadors weren't on the average citizen's radar. *Lucien must have known though,* Acadia thought to herself, grimacing.

Arnion had finished eating and brushed the crumbs off his shirt. "We've got to head back and warn everyone. The storm seems to have spent itself, and it should be dawn soon."

As he began shifting toward the exit, Acadia caught his shoulder in her calloused hand.

"How are you feeling now? Is your spirit…"

She hesitated at a loss for the right words. Arnion smiled at her, and she felt a syna like a brilliant green and purple butterfly flutter across her mind.

"I'm better now, Acadia. Thank you."

With that, he crawled out of the crevice, scanning the area carefully with both his eyes and his spirit. They were safe for the moment. No one seemed to have ventured out in the predawn after the sandstorm.

Arnion stretched his arms up toward the sky, groaning happily after being confined in such tight space. He pulled his arms behind his back until he could feel the muscles strain for a moment before releasing them.

*It's good to be alive,* he thought to himself, rolling his shoulders.

He didn't have time for a full report to Elyon, but he sent a brief message. <Lucien has discovered trividium here in Gehenna. Be in contact again soon.>

Then he ducked down and stuck his head back inside the crevice.

"It's safe, Acadia. Come on out."

He heard her shuffling around and planted his feet firmly on either side of the opening and stretched his hand down. When he felt her rough fingers firmly grasp his, he helped pull her out.

Acadia was surprised by the effortless way he seemed to lift her.

*Has Arnion always been that strong?*

Her mind flashed back to the day that he had carried Agatha through the crowds even with his limp. But Agatha was a frail wisp of a person. In the past, Acadia would have laughed at the idea of gentleness and strength together.

*What was strength but power to hold sway over others?* But now, she wondered, *Was Arnion able to be gentle because he was so strong?*

Her train of thought broke as she felt Arnion tug on her hand.

"Come on, chimad, we've got to start heading back."

# Chapter 18

Acadia wasn't sure how they slipped back into the quarry. It all seemed to pass in a blur, probably owing to some kind of spirit ability on Arnion's part. One moment, they were walking in the desert wastes. She was soaking in the most gorgeous sunrise of reds and purples she had ever seen, tugging and swinging Arnion's arm like a little girl. The next, they were somehow among the crowd of workers in the kelsum quarry surrounded by dust and the ringing of pickaxes on stone. No one had noticed their absence.

Acadia stopped swinging their joined hands as familiar bitterness of stone grit set her teeth on edge, leaching away her joy.

"I'll come for you soon," Arnion whispered in her ear. His breath was so close that it made her shiver. "Act normal, and wait for me."

Despite his limping stride, he melted into the crowd as if his body was made of nothing more than mist. Acadia blinked and scanned the area around him, but he was gone. Nothing even hinted at his passage through the swarms of prisoners.

*He must be cloaking his movements,* Acadia thought to herself. *Arnion can be so reckless,* she fretted.

Without realizing it, she began scratching at the itchy sores between her fingers. After a satisfying moment of replacing the itch with a warm burning sensation, Acadia recognized what she was doing and forced herself to stop.

*I've got to trust him,* she urged herself, pressing her palms into her thighs.

The temptation to panic, just like her temptation to scratch, was almost irresistible, but somehow, she managed to stagger over to the supply cage. Acadia grabbed a pickaxe, its handle worn smooth by the countless suffering of others who came before her.

*And others who will come long after I'm gone unless Arnion can put a stop to it somehow,* she thought grimly.

The day passed in agonizing slowness. Acadia kept waiting for another explosion or a burst of guards dragging Arnion up to the compound shouting that they'd finally found the cursed ambassador. However, everything seemed to be proceeding along like a normal day in Gehenna. The guards shouted and cussed at their laziness. Whips and bludgeon sticks sang out occasionally, but as the sun rose higher in the sky, their tormentors lost interest.

She did notice covered wagons frequently traveling back and forth from the compound to the area of yesterday's explosion. They were making an effort to be inconspicuous, she realized. If she hadn't been actively looked for them, it was doubtful she would have even noticed.

Acadia hummed to herself as she thought, *Lucien is playing his cards close to his chest for the moment. He's going out of his way to deflect any curiosity or interest, not that there's a high likelihood of that anyway down in his quarries.*

She felt a hand on her shoulder, startling her from her reverie. Arnion was beside her.

"Acadia, it's time."

She nodded and tried to swallow the lump in her throat. It was finally time to hear Arnion's plan for rescuing them. Acadia held his hand tightly as he guided her through the crowd. More people had massed together today than at any of the previous gatherings. It seemed like many of Gehenna's citizens wanted to hear what Arnion had to say.

*Even with Arnion's shield, someone is bound to notice,* Acadia fretted. *How can the guards not recognize half of their workforce is missing? Even Lucien will be able to tell something is wrong from his iron tower in the compound. We're too conspicuous.*

As if sensing her thoughts, Arnion squeezed her hand.

"Don't worry, chimad. You promised you'd trust me," he whispered before clambering on top of a boulder and holding his arms out to the assembly.

The people waited silently, standing shoulder to shoulder. Their attention was rapt. Arnion wore an unusually serious expression today. The smiles that greeted his appearance melted away to looks of concern.

"My friends, thank you for coming to hear me out. We have worked together in Lucien's quarries side by side. Though I am not a prisoner, I have seen your pain and shared in your suffering. I do not call you friends lightly for I know the promises that have been taken from you. So when I ask you to listen carefully to these tidings I bring, I trust you will.

"Yesterday, Lucien discovered a weapon of great evil that he will unleash upon Eiren and the world. We must leave Gehenna now before he is able to use it against us and prevent our escape."

Murmurs of doubt swept through the crowd. As if sensing the people's agitation, Arnion spoke more gently.

"The time has come, my friends, to leave this wretched place."

Acadia was not surprised to see Has and Eril shouldering their way through the crowd to the front. Has clasped her right arm in greeting and raised his eyebrows questioningly at her.

*Clearly, Arnion hadn't given them any more details.*

She shook her head and saw the older man's shoulders shrug in disappointment. Eril placed his hands on Arnion's boulder beseechingly.

"Arnion, please, you have to tell us what's going on. The people are scared. They don't understand."

Arnion looked down at his friend's face, eyes crinkled in a small smile before turning to face the crowd once more. In a loud voice, he declared, "I am Arnion, a citizen of Eiren, an ambassador of King Elyon, sent to negotiate your release."

The murmuring among the people grew louder. Some sadly shook their heads as whispers of "He's the ambassador!" and "So he's the one Lucien has been searching for" swam through the air.

Acadia clenched her fists.

*Well, he'd done it now. Arnion told them who he was, trusting his life to the most downtrodden and desperate rabble on the planet. Surely, they would turn him in for an extra scrap of moldy bread.*

She held her breath and scrunched her eyes shut, listening for the telltale sound of trampling feet as they all rushed to the compound, fighting to be the first one to identify him.

But the sound didn't come. Acadia cautiously squinted one eye open and then the other to find that so far everyone had stayed put. She did a quick scan. No one was rushing up to Lucien's compound or the guard shacks in the frenzy she expected. She let out a breath she didn't realize she had been holding.

*It seems I'm not the only one who's been changed by Arnion's gentle strength.*

The people were still listening, but there was a tremor of fear that ran through them now. Some were shaking, while others wrapped their arms around themselves as if seeking comfort. Arnion continued his address to them.

"Long ago, Lucien was also a citizen of Eiren, but he was cast out for his cruelty and pride. Deep within the earth, he had discovered trividium, the powerful weapon whose blast rocked the walls of this quarry yesterday. Once he is able to extract the power he needs from its essence, we will all be in grave danger. This is why I come to you now, my friends, to tell you we must leave."

A voice shouted up from the crowd. "Well, if Eiren's so great, why have they abandoned us all these years?"

Mutters and grunts of agreement rose to follow.

Holding out his hand, Arnion gently responded, "Eiren has never abandoned you. Long ago when Elorah was young, Eiren and all the other nations lived in harmony. Our rulers shared our knowledge of the spirit, and there was peace.

"Over time, the interests of our countries drifted apart. Though we remained peaceable, our relationships among the other people began to grow distant. When Lucien fell, he began a tireless campaign to alienate Eiren from the other nations. He has been working to turn the hearts and minds of Avathys, Dardak, and Kifu against us. And this is only what the Eirenian analysts have been able to detect so far. The Deceiver will not be content with the destruction of Eiren. No one on Elorah is safe while he roams free."

"But how are we supposed to stop him? We're still in debt. The Heartless King has us bound to him," a man shouted up at him. "He'll never release us before we've paid."

Arnion held up his hand, and any further outcries were silenced. His posture exuded confidence and courage. Acadia marveled at how he could project such peace into an agitated crowd with a single gesture.

"I am going to negotiate your release," he said boldly.

There were no more questions after that. Arnion slid off the rock and began the walk up the hill to the compound. The people silently followed after him, eyes wide with hope and fear.

"Come on. Let's go up to die with him then," Eril said mournfully, looking at the ground.

Acadia frowned at him, but before she could respond, Has bumped him with his shoulder.

"Come young 'un. Have a little more faith in yer friends. Didn't Arnion say to trust?"

Eril looked up at the older man's face, and Acadia was shocked to see him blinking back tears.

"Yes, Has, you're right. If anyone can do this, it's Arnion." He gestured to the procession snaking its way up the hillside. "And even if not, it's been a good run," he muttered under his breath.

Acadia hissed at his comment and moved to strike him, but Has blocked her arm.

"We can't be fightin' amongst ourselves now, lassie. Arnion is goin' to need all our strength."

Acadia shook him off and walked ahead of them, spitting fiercely on the ground.

The march proceeded up the hill. It was a very startled rear guard who jumped up from their posts as the crowd forced its way back into the compound a good half a day early. One of them ran to report to their commander, while the other two held their spears uncertainly, eying the assembly of hundreds.

# CHAPTER 19

Section Chief Kilzorn didn't sign up for this. When the requisitioner had found him staked outside the little mountain village of Liipa for savagely beating his young son to death, the negotiations had been brief.

"I gather that you enjoy using your brute strength against others weaker than yourself."

The man was a tall, willowy stranger with a lilting accent. Even before he spoke, the graceful loping strides he used to approach the holding stake gave away his foreign origins.

Kilzorn had shrugged partly because it was true and partly because he was bound and gagged by his village tribunal awaiting a possibly lethal and certainly unpleasant judgment. He hadn't meant to kill the child. It just wouldn't stop its incessant yammering and crying until Kilzorn lost what little patience he carried and struck it again and again until it was silent. Usually, its mother took it with her to the rocky field behind their shanty. She had been ill lately, skin turning sallow as it stretched taunt over her bones.

Her sister, Mot, had come from the neighboring village of Cryn to care for her during the tribunal. Whenever she passed by his stake, her eyes took on the cold glassy stare of a corpse after Kilzorn gutted it, and she would not meet his gaze. So here he crouched, cold and hungry, while Mot tried to coax a thin gruel down his shriveled wife's throat. He could smell it, the odor drifting down the hill. Kilzorn's stomach rumbled.

The stranger must have noticed his eyes wandering up the hill and cleared his throat. Kilzorn met his gaze.

"The tribunal has almost reached its decision on how best to punish you. Would you like to know how the vote is split?"

Kilzorn groaned, and the man's lips curved into a malevolent, gloating grin.

"It's fifty-fifty. Some want to cut off your hands and feet and leave you crippled. Others want to bury you up to your neck near the fire wasp grove. It appears you're rather unpopular around here. Not terribly surprising, really." His face wrinkled in distaste for a moment before he pulled out a thin white cloth and held it over his nose and mouth.

It wasn't anything the condemned man didn't already know. Kilzorn had stared coolly at the stranger as if to remind him that if he wasn't bound, the conversation would be going very differently.

The man crept closer and whispered in his ear, "Would you like to change that?"

Naturally, Kilzorn had agreed. It wasn't as if he had many other options at the moment. Solis, as he later learned the requisitioner was called, promised him a job where he could beat on helpless pathetic people all day long and get praised for it.

"It's right up your alley, Kilzorn, really. The more ruthless you are, the further you'll go with Lucien. Cruelty is like an art form with him. He's a true master."

After that, it hadn't taken much. A couple bags of drakka shaken at the tribunal's feet and Solis's blood oath that Kilzorn would never again set foot in the country of Ulekruw, let alone the hills of Liipa, and he was freed.

"I didn't expect it to be that easy." Kilzorn muttered, rubbing his sore wrists where the bindings had chaffed.

"You know what they say?" Solis laughed. "Money talks. That and a little name dropping of the entity I represent. They were so anxious for us to disappear. I wondered if they were going to pay *us* to leave."

He spritzed something from a small jar into his handkerchief and breathed in deeply, sighing. It was doubtful that things were as simple as Solis described. Kilzorn imagined that he had dropped some substantial threats along with his gold when he went to visit the elders. Solis was clearly a man used to getting his own way. At least he had been honest about the job description. The people in Gehenna were the most miserable wretches imaginable.

Kilzorn loved his job. Lashing out at these feeble creatures whenever a fit of rage took him was utterly satisfying. They were completely defenseless and at his mercy.

When he was promoted to section chief for the rear guard, he had rubbed his sweaty hands together with glee. Pounding on people was hard work when you put effort into it like he did. A section chief had to set the example after all. And the quarry was so dusty and hot. It must have been a reward for all his cruel efficiency. Lucien had promoted him after Kilzorn had put down a small commotion at the southside water bucket. At least three wretches were sent straight to the burning pits that day after knocks from his bludgeon stick.

Now, guarding the compound, Section Chief Kilzorn could relax a bit. Hazy quiet days of alcohol induced naps and helping himself to extra rations from the kitchen stretched before him far into the foreseeable future. Unless he screwed up royally and fell from Lucien's good graces, that was.

He didn't like the look of this mob straining back through the compound gates so early in the day. Kilzorn preferred fights where the odds were clearly in his favor, and confrontations with the prisoners were always in his favor. They were usually such weak, starving, pitiful creatures that he forgot they were human like himself. But they didn't look weak anymore, especially the man leading them. Despite his limping stride, he looked more ferocious than a female ungalor protecting her brood. The section chief felt a trickle of sweat run down his spine, and he shivered.

*That man scares me.*

Kilzorn didn't want to stay and confront this crowd.

*There must be hundreds of them coming up from the quarry now. What are those blasted guards doing down there?*

As the most senior officer present, he needed to report this anomalous situation straight to Lucien himself. Kilzorn wasn't crazy about that task either. His illustrious lord had a tendency to vent his wrath on the bearers of unpleasant news.

Still, he found himself hustling down the hall. It couldn't quite be called a sprint. In his years of working at Gehenna, his muscles had grown soft, swallowed in a comfortable layer of fat. The prisoners may be starving, but the guards certainly weren't. Kilzorn puffed down the cement walkway through the columns of gray pillars that lined the central courtyard. When he reached the stairs that led to the upper levels, he took a pause to catch his breath. Wheezing, he placed his hands on his knees and bent over. The hot dusty air did nothing to help refresh him, so he shook it off and started making his way up the stairs.

*Something's not right. I need to notify Lucien as soon as possible. Perhaps if I'm quick enough, I'll be able to save my own neck at the very least.*

Motivated by these thoughts, the section chief found his second wind on the landing just one flight below the third floor. He braced himself along the wall with his meaty hand and charged up the final steps and down the hall. As he neared the seemingly innocuous metal door, three doors down the hall on the left, Kilzorn slowed his pace. He needed a few seconds to catch his breath or risk his report coming out as a series of hysterical and inarticulate gasping noises.

In his chambers, Lucien was pouring over a map of the border between Eiren and Gehenna.

"They're certain to build defenses here and here," he muttered to himself, tapping at two elevated ridges that rose up sharply from a riverbed.

With the discovery of trividium, finally he could begin moving his pawns into place. Looking at a stretch of low open ground, he rubbed his temple thoughtfully. "Now, this area will be a little more challenging for us to hold. Perhaps if we sent a company up along the right and used these men simply as a diversion…"

There was a knock at the door. Lucien dropped his charcoal nib with a sigh. These guards were so worthless, always interrupting him right in the middle of a brilliant train of thought. He had half a mind to slaughter all of them and start the training program from scratch.

*It's so hard to find good help these days. Why can't more people be vicious and intelligent?*

Lucien ran both hands through his shoulder-length mane of hair and leaned back in his chair.

"Enter," he snapped in annoyance.

The metal door creaked open, and Kilzorn hesitantly stuck his head inside. He accidentally caught Lucien's gaze for a moment and was met with a fierce scowl before he bowed his head humbly.

"Begging your pardon, Your Grace. I know you didn't want to be disturbed unless it was urgent, but the prisoners, they are—" He stopped abruptly as Lucien held up his hand.

"Tut, tut, Kilzorn." Lucien spoke with mocking reproach. "How many times do I have to remind you, Gehenna has citizens, not prisoners."

He crossed around to the front of his battle table and approached his quivering guard at the door. Kilzorn was sweating profusely. The section chief entered fully into the room and knelt before his approaching master, surreptitiously wiping his palms on his thighs on the way down. He stared at the fibers woven together to form the plush cords of the black carpet on the floor. Impossibly, it didn't appear to have a speck of dust on it.

Kilzorn swallowed and said weakly, "Yes, Your Worshipfulness, but—"

"Say it."

Lucien was standing directly over him now. His voice was dangerously soft. Kilzorn could see his glossy patent leather shoes shinning up at him. They didn't have a speck of dust on them either. Kilzorn wanted to laugh at the absurdity of it. He was probably about to die, and here he was admiring his master's astonishing cleanliness in probably the dirtiest place on the planet.

"The citizens, my lord," Kilzorn managed to choke out.

Looking down at his terrified section chief, it pleased Lucien to remember he could inspire such fear so easily. He laughed and said cheerfully, "There now, that wasn't so hard, was it?" He even went so far as to knock Kilzorn on the shoulder playfully and got another thrill when the guard flinched as if he was about to be beheaded.

*Now, I remember why I keep these guards around*, he mused to himself. *They're such fun to play with. Big lumbering beasts who roll over in submission when faced with a true predator.* "Now, what was it you came to report?"

Kilzorn thought his heart was going to burst out of his chest. At least three times now, his life had passed before his eyes, but Lucien seemed in a good humor for the moment.

*Maybe I can survive this if I get the news out quickly and flee.* "It's the citizens, Your Grace. They're acting strangely. They've all stopped working and started coming back into the compound. They're a—"

He was interrupted as Lucien's fist slammed into the left side of his temple and sent him sprawling to the ground.

"What did you say?"

Lucien grabbed the collar of his shirt and hauled Kilzorn to his feet. The guard stammered in terror and started to urinate. Lucien tossed him to the side in disgust and strode to one of the windows that opened into the courtyard. He ripped open the slatted wooden shutters with such force that the walls shook and gazed down with contempt.

*Tsk, so that guard wasn't exaggerating,* he thought. *What ridiculous problem had their incompetence led to now? Perhaps once I've sorted this mess out, I really will go through their barracks and kill them all. Call it stress relief.*

Lucien smirked at the thought and checked himself briefly in the full-length standing mirror he kept in his office.

*It wouldn't do to look slovenly. Keeping up appearances is important after all.*

Satisfied, he grinned back at his reflection. Reaching for his bright-red general's cloak, Lucien threw it over his shoulders, fabric whirling as he closed the door.

# CHAPTER 20

The unusual sight that met him at the entrance to the courtyard would have had a lesser man gaping in shock, but Lucien was no such man. He prided himself on his self-control, not allowing even the slightest ripple of surprise to wink across his expression. Gazing smoothly across the collection of his workers, he stifled the urge to raise an eyebrow.

The rabble seemed to cross both gender and age divides. In the past, brief insurrections had risen, usually a group of meat-headed young men who thought they could press him into bargaining.

*Fools.*

Their demise was always excruciating and absolute.

*Although now that I think of it,* the Heartless King mused, *perhaps I should start leaving one or two alive to tell the tale. It might save me the time of having to put down similar efforts in the future.*

Lucien was pleased by the fear he felt pouring off those gathered. He held out his arms to the crowd like a wounded father as he drew closer.

"My pets, what reason could you have for this blatant show of disobedience?" He admonished them. Conjuring an expression of betrayed reproach, he made eye contact with as many as possible. "I'm so disappointed in you." Lucien was pleased that none of them could return his gaze.

*Revolting sheep.*

He despised them. Yet, as his eyes scanned the crowd, enhanced with the malicious intent of his spirit, there was one who glared back at him, defiant.

*Well, well, what have we here?* Lucien thought to himself. *A scruffy little leader, perhaps?*

He treaded nearer to the would-be insurgent, curious. The man was young, not surprising, and he seemed totally unaffected by Lucien's spiritual menace accompanying his scrutiny. Most fell to their knees quivering or, at the very least, felt uncomfortable enough to look away.

*Not this man, practically still a boy really.*

The youth was dirty and unremarkable. Clothed in the typical rags of his workers, Lucien never would have picked him out as a potential leader or threat based on his appearance. The smoke rash spreading across his features marred his face, indicating he had been here a while. And yet, he didn't appear broken. In fact, if his intense stare was any indication, he was filled with a smoldering righteous anger.

*Ah well,* Lucien thought, *I can use that, certainly. Anger is so easily manipulated.*

The leaderling approached him with such dignity and assurance. Lucien was taken aback.

"I've come to negotiate the release of those gathered here." The youth's voice rang out clearly for all to hear.

Lucien couldn't even get him to stutter as he threw a malicious wave of panic and terror from the recesses of his spirit at him. It should have at least splashed into the people around him, and yet they stood calmly by the young man, unflinching. In fact, the crowd as a whole seemed to be pulling strength from him. The lingering fear from Lucien's arrival was melting away.

This was no citizen of Gehenna.

*But that could only mean...*

Lucien had to be sure. Wrapping his disdain around himself like a scarf, he sneered, "On whose authority do you initiate these negotiations?"

His nostrils flared. It was the only indication that Lucien was barely able to control his rage. The thought that this pathetic worm could disrupt his composure only infuriated Gehenna's ruler further.

The young man was like a rock, unflinching before him.

"I speak on behalf of Elyon Melek Iustus, ruler of Eiren, as his appointed ambassador to Gehenna."

It was just as the Heartless King suspected. *An ambassador. And this one seemed to have considerable power.*

Still, Lucien had beaten ambassadors before. He had a perfect track record for sniffing them out and destroying them. It gave him immense satisfaction to foil Elyon's foolish schemes and motivated his people toward further loyalty.

*A win-win.*

Lucien smirked at the young man and casually brushed some imaginary dust from his shoulder.

"Well, I must say, this is a first. Usually, my pets drag ambassadors up here kicking and screaming. I'm quite impressed by the awe they're exhibiting toward you. How *did* you manage to frighten them enough to keep their hands off?" Whatever game this little leaderling was playing, Lucien would catch him at it and expose him.

"It's not fear, Lucien," the youth replied. "It's trust. Something you would know little about."

"Now, now, there's no need to begin hurling insults," Lucien chided. "As you can see, you have me at a disadvantage. You've riled up my workforce with false promises and brought a mob to the very gates of my house. Not very sporting, is it ambassador?"

The youth's eyes blazed. "I should kill you where you stand for what I've seen you do here." He clenched his hands tightly and took a deep breath. "But today, my main priority is getting these people to safety. If you allow us to go peaceably, I'll allow you to live."

"How magnanimous of you." Lucien did a mock bow. At the same instant, he sent a poisonous jolt streaking out of his spirit. It flanked around to the right and came up on the youth from behind. And then—nothing.

Acadia felt the hair stand up on the back of her neck. Outwardly, it looked like nothing much was happening. Arnion had revealed himself to Lucien and ordered their release, even threatening Lucien's life. Normally, she would have slapped herself in the forehead in the face of such foolishness, but she was currently too terrified. Gehenna's leader had responded with scorn to Arnion's demands. They were still speaking to one another calmly.

*So why do I have such a strong feeling of apprehension curling around my stomach like a vice?*

Reaching into her spirit, Acadia sent out a questioning tendril. An otherworldly scene flashed before her eyes, and she rocked backward, almost falling over. Using her spirit, she could see what looked like two massive windstorms, one swirling around Arnion and the other around Lucien. While Arnion's radiated a pure white light, Lucien's vortex was a dark mahogany red, close to black.

Lucien spoke, and he must have been using his spirit, because his voice was amplified. It sounded like a thousand hateful voices screaming inside her head.

<Insolent cur! How dare you seek to challenge me on the very seat of my power.>

The sound froze the blood in her veins. Acadia put her hands over her ears, but she could not drown out the sound of his voice.

The winds around Gehenna's ruler surged toward Arnion with murderous intent. Just as the racing storm seemed about to consume him, the ambassador raised his right arm and gave a small flick with his wrist, sending it swirling harmlessly off to the right.

<Nothing here is yours by right. Everything you have was achieved by artifice and betrayal.> Arnion spoke, and Acadia was bewildered to hear that his voice also undulated with power like the sound of rushing waters. His eyes, usually so gentle, blazed pure white with crackling energy. Streaks of lightning like arrows shot forth from the white storm blazing around him.

*There must be thousands of them,* Acadia thought, *burning white hot.*

She could feel the intense heat radiating off the arrows as they arced upward and then plummeted down onto Lucien. The Heartless King howled as the burning arrows pierced through his shield and rained down upon him. He swatted at them with his hands, crying out as his flesh was singed. Driven down to his knees, he curled up trying to protect his head.

Acadia felt numb with terror. The forces at work here were so far beyond her. The power displayed by both Arnion and Lucien made her tremble. Of course, she had known that Lucien was powerful, but she never could have dreamed of power like this. Arnion, behind that cheerful voice and crinkled smile, was also carrying a secret. Acadia wished that she could somehow disengage herself from what was happening, but her spirit and her gaze seemed stuck in place.

Just when she thought she was about to see Lucien torn to pieces, he held up his hands and implored in a loud voice, <You condemn me for artifice and betrayal, and yet here you assault me and attempt to steal my workforce unprovoked, polluting their minds to rebel against me, their rightful master.> His voice hiccupped with a suppressed sob of pain.

Arnion hesitated for a moment and then drew his hand back slightly. The gleaming arrows froze in place, hovering above Lucien's head. <It was not unprovoked as you well know. However, I am amenable to a less combative form of negotiation.>

Arnion clenched his hand closed, and the barrage flickered out of existence like a snuffed candle flame. The white energy faded out of his eyes, and Acadia strove to see what color they were. Usually, they were so swollen with smoke rash that she could never really tell. Before she could get the chance, she was yanked back into the physical world. Jolted by the sudden transition, she swayed woozily.

Lucien seemed to be faring worse than her. Whatever had happened between his spirit and Arnion's spirit had taken a physical toll. He staggered backward against a pillar and braced himself against it with one arm. His breath came out in great gasps, and his muscles spasmed.

# CHAPTER 21

With effort, the Heartless King pulled himself up into a standing position. However, he still leaned heavily on one of the thick stone pillars that supported the upper galleries around the courtyard.

Turning to face Arnion, Lucien spat out, "Even if you kill me, they'll never be free. They've entered into a blood oath. Every last one." He wiped his mouth with his sleeve and chuckled under his breath.

Arnion was sure he misheard. *A blood oath?* The prince's thoughts raced. *How could he possibly...with this many people? It should be impossible.*

For the first time since slipping across the border to Gehenna, the ambassador felt fear, though not for himself. Gehenna's citizens were more deeply ensnared than he could ever have imagined.

"I can see by your expression that you realize what this means." Lucien cackled. His normally resonate voice was distorted, laced with pain. "Only a blood payment can release them, and they haven't paid nearly enough. They'll never be free, not till every last drop has been drained from their bodies."

Lucien roared in spiteful laughter. Foamy white spittle flecked the corners of his mouth. Frantically, he licked his lips before being seized in a fit of giggling. With difficulty, Lucien managed to stifle his glee long enough to whisper, "They won't get out till they've paid the last drakka." His eyes blazed with maniacal hatred. Gradually, the Heartless King seemed able to draw the shreds of composure around himself once more. He smoothed back the hair that had fallen out of place.

"Even with all that power, there's nothing you can do to save them. You're too late." He snickered and held his hand up in mock angst for theatrical effect.

It felt as if the world had fallen out from beneath Arnion's feet. He could never have imagined that Lucien had the strength or determination to bind thousands of people to himself with blood oaths.

*Probably more than a million if you counted all the lives that had been tragically lost over the years of his reign,* the Eirenian thought sadly.

Even the weight of one blood oath took its toll on a normal person. A load of this magnitude should have overwhelmed him to the point where his mind broke, and he was reduced to drooling and rolling around in the dust. Yet from the display he was putting on, Lucien did not appear to feel the burden at all. It was as if he had severed the link from his consciousness somehow.

The muscles in Arnion's throat clenched. Sweat beaded his brow.

<Father.> He cried out with his spirit, sending his desperate plea hurtling across the distance that separated him from his kingdom. <Father, help me, please.>

Physical time around him seemed to slow almost to a complete stop, the world frozen in place. Arnion reached for his father and instantly felt the soothing presence of Elyon respond. Flickering back and forth like bolts of electricity, their thoughts raced to and fro in nanoseconds, an entire conversation conducted in the span of a human heartbeat.

<I am here, my son.>

Arnion drew in a deep breath. Just feeling his father's reply gave him a measure of peace. He wasn't alone. <Father, I've found my chimad.>

<Oh?>

Although brief, the echo of Elyon's spirit radiated warmth. His father was pleased. This only made Arnion want to wring his hands in despair. He tried to suppress his emotions from spilling out in a syna that would alarm the king. It was like trying to hold onto a ska-klop slick with pond mucus. Somehow, he succeeded.

<But, Father, she, like all of them here…they're tied to Lucien with a blood oath. He'll never release them, never be satisfied until they are dead.> Arnion felt his control slipping and blinked back tears. It was an impossible situation. <There is more. The council's suspicions have been confirmed. Lucien has continued searching for trividium, and now, he has discovered a vein of it right here in Gehenna. I believe he plans to use it on the people bound to him. They must be evacuated.>

A wave of peace washed over Arnion. It carried away the swells of paralyzing fear that were threatening to engulf him. He could think clearly again. Elyon was comforting him.

Despite the encouragement he was sending his son, Eiren's king was deeply troubled. <It was our greatest fear that Lucien should discover more of that cursed element. We never imagined his power had grown so great that he could bind this magnitude of people to him. Yet you say that he is not overcome.>

Arnion narrowed his eyes. <Not in the least.>

He felt his father's gentle voice surrounded him once more.

<What will you do, my son?>

A silence stretched briefly across the distance. Elyon let out a deep sigh, closing his eyes. He knew what was coming.

<I'm going to do what I was sent here to do. I'm going to free these people by paying their debt. It's the only way.> Arnion's voice was firm. Once he recognized the way he needed to proceed, he felt determination course through him like blood made of steel.

In Eiren, the king's eyes tightened in anguish. *My son, my only son is about to slip beyond my grasp. It is a terrible, unbearable cost. How can I allow it?*

The image of his son's bright smiling face as a child flashed through his mind, and Elyon wanted to cup the memory in his hands and preserve it forever. He remembered his son's resolve as he volunteered for this mission. Arnion had known even then what might happen, yet his eyes were filled with hope.

The prince did not offer this exchange lightly. Although Elyon could feel the father heart inside him breaking, as king he knew that freeing the captives in Gehenna and breaking that madman's stranglehold were top priority. He also knew that his son's beloved was down in those quarries and that Arnion would lay down his life to free her.

<Very well, Ambassador. Eiren will not interfere.>

For a moment, Elyon swore he could feel his son's arms encircle him in an embrace.

<Thank you, Father.> If Arnion had been speaking with his natural voice, it would have been raw with sorrow. <I love you.>

Elyon felt tears trickling down from the corners of his eyes, but he made no move to brush them away. <I love you too, my son.> He felt Arnion sever the connection, and the king of the mightiest nation Elorah had ever known wept bitterly.

Arnion retracted his spirit and returned his complete focus to the deranged ruler before him. Lucien should have been able to sense at least in part what had transpired, but he was too distracted by his weakened spiritual state and his jeering to notice. The ambassador breathed a sigh of relief. Having an element of surprise might give him the added leverage he needed to pull this off. It didn't look like it would take much to knock Lucien off-balance at the moment. Locking eyes with the Heartless King, Arnion took a step forward.

"Blood for blood. I offer you my life in place of theirs."

# CHAPTER 22

It wasn't an unheard-of proposition, taking on a blood oath for another. But this was usually reserved for extreme cases, aging family members, lovers, and the infirm.

*I shouldn't be surprised that one of those insufferable fools would offer up himself like this.*

Lucien pondered his options. He would have liked to stride around his office for a bit. It always helped his thoughts flow. Then perhaps, he would lean back in his joffa chair and smoke his kelta pipe, thinking through all the options. Unfortunately, the circumstances called for a rapid decision, and Lucien hated to be too hasty.

*This ambassador is strong, stronger than any opponent I've faced in a long time. Strong enough that he could prove a formidable obstacle to my plans if left unchecked. And why shouldn't I allow him to nobly sacrifice himself like this?* Lucien mused. *Not that it would do my dear citizens any good I'm afraid.*

The Heartless King forced himself to cough, effectively cutting off another series of nearly irrepressible giggling.

*That fool is under the assumption I've bound them all to me, that his blood will be an acceptable substitute. In a way, I should be flattered that the Eirenians assume I'm capable of holding on to so many contract threads at one time. Delicious really, their naivete. All it takes is a little tweaking of the contract here, a little twisting of the binding there, and you get something else entirely.*

It was not the first time that Lucien was grateful for his careful study of legislature in his younger days. You needed to know the rules before you could bend them to suit your needs. The Heartless King took great joy in his use of subterfuge. It wasn't just anyone who could manipulate Elorah's complex contract system so perfectly.

*Elyon, you really went all out this time, didn't you?* Lucien was exuberant.

*You finally sent someone who actually has a chance to stop me, and yet his pathetic sentimentality will be his downfall, just as yours will be. I'm going to enjoy killing this man.*

*Then as you watch his death from your ivory towers, you will see that nothing has changed. No one will be free, and this great champion of yours will have died in vain. I wish that I could see your face when you finally realize how hopeless your situation is. Elyon, watch as I tear the kingdom from your hands brick by brick.*

*Everything is finally coming together,* Lucien crowed in his mind. *This troublesome annoyance will soon be concluded, and as an added benefit, the death of another ambassador should motivate my dear citizens to put out their best efforts in the crucial weeks ahead.*

As soon as Arnion had uttered his proposal, Acadia ruthlessly tugged on his arm.

"What are you saying," she hissed under her breath. "Arnion, are you crazy?"

He turned to face her, and her eyes widened in shock. Her lunatic was smiling.

"You don't know what Lucien is capable of! Don't even think about handing yourself over to him!"

Arnion gently tugged his arm from her grasp. "Acadia, listen to me—"

She couldn't bare the look in his eyes. Acadia began shaking her head back and forth. Her chest hurt. It felt as if her entire body was filled with lead, and there was an irritating fuzziness to her vision.

"No. No!" She wouldn't let him finish. Acadia furiously tore her hand from his grasp and swiped at her eyes.

*This can't be happening,* her mind pleaded.

He took her face and gently held it between his palms. "Acadia, listen to me—"

"No!"

She jerked her head, trying to twist out of his grasp. Her eyes met his, and startled by the distress pooling in his normally cheerful expression, she stopped struggling.

"You don't understand," she entreated. She would make a spectacle of herself, fall weeping at his feet, if only that would get him to stop this dreadful exchange. "Whatever pledge he makes, Lucien won't honor it."

"I understand your fear, Acadia, but properly executed, a blood oath can be transferred to another. Even Lucien can't stop that." Even in a whisper, his voice was soothing. He spoke to her like one would speak to a frightened sagrin to keep it from charging.

Acadia wanted to wrap her arms around herself and rock back and forth. Arnion didn't understand. Lucien wasn't capable of mercy or goodness. He would do everything in his power to make sure they all suffered bitterly till the end. There was nothing Arnion could do to change that.

"Please." Her voice warbled as she reached out a tremulous hand to clutch at the sleeve of his shirt.

"Acadia." His hands moved from her face to her shoulders, and he shook her gently as if trying to release her from the knot of fear and panic that was wrapping itself around her heart. "Listen to me."

*His voice is so steady,* she marveled to herself. *How can his voice be so calm at a time like this?*

He waited for her to fix her eyes on him once more.

*So patient,* she thought. She wondered if she was having an emotional breakdown.

"I love you."

His voice was hushed, but to Acadia, it might as well have been a shout. Everything else in the background faded away, and her mind replayed those three words over and over. Her mouth opened, speechless.

Arnion would have chuckled at her goggle-eyed stare, but this was not a moment for levity. He pressed his lips close to her ear. "I love you, Acadia. Trust me. You're going to get out of here, and I need you to remember that."

Before she could pull together a coherent argument, he kissed her forehead and turned toward Eril on his right.

"Take care of her."

Eril nodded wordlessly and stepped up beside her, eyes tight. Has held out his right arm, and Arnion took it, gripping his forearm tightly. The ambassador met his gaze without flinching.

"It's time."

Has bowed his head and let go.

"If you're quite finished with your little scene," Lucien taunted.

He peered closer at the creature that was clutching onto the ambassador as if for dear life. "Oh my! Acadia, is that you?" he called out. His eyes glimmered with malice.

"I hardly recognized you, my little dove. Even in your diminished state, I see that you've managed to catch the eye of our distinguished guest. You always were a clever one."

The acid in his smile could have melted a steel vault. She shrank back from him, and the ambassador placed himself protectively in front of her, holding out his arm.

"Well, Lucien, do we have a deal?"

The rabble before the Heartless King shifted, waiting.

*It's going to be so satisfying to crush their hopes as well. How dare they even think to congregate here against me with this scrawny youth as their leader?*

Lucien was going to make them all pay, starting with the ambassador. He spread his hands wide, magnanimous.

"Noble ambassador of the Glittering City, I accept your proposal on behalf of the people of Gehenna. Your blood for their blood in a manner of my choosing."

He reached out his hand, laced with his spirit. The ambassador stepped forward to meet him, and Lucien declared in a loud voice, "Here on the sixth day of the ninth month of Salyrn, I do willingly exchange the blood vows of all those bound to me within Gehenna for the life blood of Eiren's ambassador, representative of one Elyon Melek Iustus."

Lucien shivered in anticipation. The ambassador held his gaze.

*It's going to be so delightful to shatter his self-confidence, to reduce that fearless expression to a quivering pulp of gore and tears.*

Yet for a moment looking into the youth's eyes, Lucien felt a trill of warning as if there was something he had failed to consider, a circumstance he hadn't accounted for. He brushed it aside, annoyed. The young fool would be dead soon enough. No one was strong enough to stop him anymore, not even Elyon himself.

"Do you accept these terms, ambassador?"

Arnion took his hand, and Lucien could feel the threads of the contract working through both of them, burning red cords of light that twined between their forearms and forged a knot of connection. Gehenna's king could feel the weight of it on him like a heavy chain.

"If you would accompany me to the stage, Ambassador, we can proceed with the payment."

He gestured toward the center of the courtyard. Lucien wanted to get rid of this burdensome contract as soon as possible. Feeding into the deceptive charm was draining. He wouldn't be able to keep it hidden for long.

*I need to kill this fool quickly.*

Being forced to actually negotiate terms with Eiren, even if they were deceitful and misleading terms, infuriated him to no end. He would make sure this ambassador felt his wrath sevenfold for making him appear weak in front of his own people.

# CHAPTER 23

<Urgent report for His Majesty!>

The message was frayed at the edges, a mark of anxiety on the part of its conveyor. Eirenian messengers underwent a strict training program. A large part of their selection came from the aptitude to remain calm during situations of extreme stress. Information that could trouble a sender so much was not going to be pleasant.

King Elyon leaned forward in his chair, pressing his elbows onto the ruewood desk in front of him. It was the news he had been dreading.

<Sire, multiple visio ports are reporting unusual activity in Gehenna. All its people are assembling in the compound center. Our analysts state it is unprecedented behavior at this time of day. They have identified Lucien and—>

The message twanged and skipped a beat. Elyon pressed his fingers to his right temple and took a deep breath.

<And who they believe to be the crown prince at the center of the disturbance, my lord.>

The king had already risen to his feet and was moving toward the door before the spirit communication was finished. <Have you notified the advisors?> He sent back swiftly.

<Yes, Your Majesty. This information is being relayed to them as we speak.>

The sender seemed to be regaining his calm in the wake of the more routine messenger protocols.

Elyon flung the door open in a rush, startling the unsuspecting cleaning crew in the hall. He gestured to them apologetically but did not break his rapid stride down the passageway.

Reaching out to the trailing call of the messenger, he inquired, <Which visio port has the optimal reconnaissance position?>

<The analysts are projecting port E-6 to be most advantageous at this time, my lord. I can notify you if anything changes.> The sender hesitated, unsure.

Normally, Elyon was very informal with his staff and took the time to encourage them as needed. Today, all he could manage was <very good> along with a brief syna of the royal seal. He barreled down the hall toward the East Wing, scattering those in his path.

Along the way, Advisor Maulki fell into step behind him, face grim. The king acknowledged his presence with a respectful inclination of his head, which was returned without the exchange of words. Elyon always thought that one of the clearest signs of Maulki's wisdom came from knowing when to keep silent and when to speak. He appreciated that the advisor did not attempt to lighten the mood or downplay the situation.

Visio port E-6 was accessible by gated maglift and required security class 705 or higher to operate. Although any of Eiren's top advisory council had permission to access the ports, Elyon saw a group of his council members waiting outside the maglift door. Advisors Arsk, Ayam, and Genoas bowed silently as he approached. He nodded in greeting and swept the gate open with a flick from his right hand. The advisors parted respectfully, allowing their king to enter first and then followed behind him, hands clasped tightly in front of themselves as a sign of respect.

The metal doors closed precisely without even a snick as the metal teeth folded together. The magnetic coils activated, and the maglift smoothly traveled up the three hundred floors to the visio port spire in the span of five breaths. Its passengers did not feel even the slightest effect of its motion when it stopped.

As the doors slid open, Lead Analyst Naileah was there waiting. Her silver robes indicating her position were immaculate. She and all her staff bowed deeply at the waist as the king entered the room. Two aids remained beside her, while the rest scurried quickly back to their positions at the grid screens and logistics portals.

"Welcome, Your Majesty. Section E-6 Lead Analyst Naileah at your service." She spoke with a resonant voice as pleasant as a cool stream in summertime. "We sent messengers to notify you and the council as soon as our observations were confirmed among all seven eastern flanking ports."

She paused for a moment but at the king's indication, proceeded.

"As per standing protocols, whenever an ambassador is sent into Gehenna, we have maintained a team conducting continuous surveillance in the region. Our recon agents have reported a variety of escalating circumstances beginning with the explosion one day prior."

The analyst glanced down briefly at her notes on the data pad and tapped it quickly with her stylus.

"Shortly before midday today, a large group of workers from the southwest section congregated en masse and began a march back into the central compound. No guards were observed with them. His Royal Highness, the crown prince, was believed to be leading them."

Naileah wanted to chew the end of her stylus with nerves, but she restrained herself, settling for tapping it a few times on the side of her tablet as she glanced down again. She had to make sure she got all the details exactly right. Overlooking anything, even the most unsuspecting minutia, could lead to a critical error in calculation.

"Upon entering the courtyard, the group was quickly met by Lucien and a brief spirit skirmish ensued. From our observations, the crown prince appeared to be victorious."

Naileah's stylus tapped more rapidly.

"However, Lucien has not surrendered or attempted to lay down arms. All remaining work details have been summoned back to the compound. They are gathering in the courtyard, and it appears preparations are being made for another of Lucien's heinous displays of violence."

The Lead Analyst swallowed against the dryness pressing down on her throat.

"Protocol dictates that we prepare for a worst-case extraction scenario, and you were notified immediately." *In both your royal capacity and as next of kin*, she thought grimly.

Maulki gripped King Elyon's right shoulder in solace. "Your Majesty?" he queried.

The other advisors stared at each other in disbelief. Their worst fears were being realized. Elyon patted the loyal farmer's hand and stepped forward.

"You've done well, Lead Analyst Naileah. Today, I thank you for your vigilance, not only as your king but as a father."

He held out a hand to her palm up. She curtsied low and raised her hand to meet his. It was an ancient custom of respect. Naileah was silently grateful to her mother, who had drilled royal etiquette into her from the moment she began her first position at the palace many years ago. Elyon lifted her hand to his lips and kissed it.

Naileah flushed to be paid such a high honor from the king though it was difficult to notice beneath her russet skin. Such practices were usually reserved for visiting royalty or emissaries returning from essential peacekeeping missions.

*To recognize me in such a way, the Eirenian king must be truly grateful*, she thought.

Naileah squelched the urge to bow again. It would be improper since he had acknowledged her as one to whom he was indebted.

The king squeezed her hand before releasing it. "Please continue to observe and analyze the situation." His voice was calm but heavy with sorrow. "Send notifications for a bereavement transport with two accompanying passenger conveyors and the standard security detail for border contact with Gehenna—"

"Sire!" Advisor Genoas stepped forward passionately, eyes blazing. "Forgive me for my deep impertinence, but there is still time!" He thrust out his arm like a spear toward the smudge that was Gehenna's border, his crimson robe rippling on his arm like a bloody banner. "We can send incursion craft. Not even Lucien would be prepared for the new advancements we've made in stealth combat technology. We could be in and out of there in minutes, rescuing the crown prince with minimal casualties."

Elyon put both hands on his advisor's shoulders.

"And what then, my dear friend? What will we have accomplished?" The king's voice was resigned. "We will still have war with

Gehenna, helpless people sacrificed as bloody pawns in a battle with a rabid madman."

Maulki looked at the other advisor with reproach. "Please forgive Genoas for his breech of etiquette, my lord. But we are all deeply concerned for the crown prince. Surely, you don't intend to stand back and do nothing?"

The advisor's normally placid eyes were troubled. King Elyon met his gaze.

"Arnion has entered into a blood oath with Lucien on behalf of the people of Gehenna. The prince has already contacted me personally about it."

Naileah flinched and dropped her data pad. It shattered on the floor, and her stylus rolled away under a technician's chair.

For a moment, everyone in E-6 seemed to pause as the weight of what the king had revealed sunk in. They knew how merciless Lucien would be in extracting his payment, and yet it was a testament to the crown prince's power that the Heartless King could be forced to concede any ground at all, especially where his workforce was concerned.

Naileah knelt on the ground and began collecting the pieces of her data pad, tears falling from her eyes. Not for the equipment, it auto synched with the main information hub every five breaths so no critical information was lost. She wept for the crown prince, who was beloved by all of Eiren.

*What a terrible cost! How can the king bear it?* she silently wondered. *Are those people even capable of comprehending what will be paid on their behalf?*

Her thoughts drifted bitterly for a moment before a technician crouched before her, holding her stylus in a trembling hand.

"Thank you," she whispered with a watery smile.

Iridescent robes tumbled around her, and it took Naileah a moment to realize the king of her nation was kneeling down to help her up.

"I thank you for your compassion, my child," he spoke to her softly. Then louder, he addressed the room. "No one feels the burden of this tragic situation more deeply than me. However, Arnion and I are in agreement that it must be done. I have given my word as king that Eiren will not interfere."

Naileah looked helplessly down at the shards of the tablet in her hands.

*He's asking us all to let the prince die when we could save him. Based on what I've observed during that skirmish earlier, Arnion doesn't even need us. If he wanted to, he could easily have taken Lucien's head. Yet he's choosing to willingly lay down his life.*

The crown prince's bravery lit a fire in her blood. She snapped to attention, still holding the broken pieces of her tablet in front of her.

Turning to the aid on her left, she said with authority, "Please take this to the tech maintenance bay. Maybe they can repair it." Then to the aid on her right, she added, "Please find me another model C0-812 tablet. There should be one or two charging in the storage locker."

Glancing around the room, Naileah clapped her hands.

"All right, people, you heard His Majesty! We are moving to recon level 10. We may not be moving in to assist, but by shreeve, we are going to give His Majesty and the crown prince the best possible intelligence we can offer. This is what we have been training for. I want everyone at full capacity today."

"Yes, ma'am!" a chorus of her staff responded.

The Lead Analyst's energy and purpose broke the choke hold of despair that had invaded the room. Minor analysts, messengers, grid screen technicians, and logistics staff set about their work with renewed vigor. If their king had to watch this nightmare unfold, by shreeve, they were going to give everything they had to support him.

Realizing the impolite expression that had slipped out, Naileah gasped slightly and covered her mouth. With a low curtsy, she whispered, "Pardon the language, Your Majesty."

She wanted to close her eyes and melt into the floor, but she settled on biting the corner of her lip. King Elyon nodded at Naileah, and his eyes shone with gratitude.

"I thought the speech very fitting."

He smiled at her. Advisor Maulki turned to face the Lead Analyst, touching two fingers to his heart and then his forehead in an Eirenian gesture of solidarity and fidelity. All of the staff in visio port E-6 repeated the sign. After a moment of internal struggle, Advisor Genoas in his garnet robes humbly bowed his head and followed suit.

# CHAPTER 24

Lucien's guards had spent most of the day in a state of paralyzed shock. Dazed, they watched as the prisoners marched back into the compound and were dismayed to find they could not lift a finger to stop them. It was as if their bodies had fallen asleep, a mass of numb, tingly limbs that no longer responded to brain signals.

Trembling, they watched as their fearless leader seemed to crumble right before their eyes. A few words of banter between him and a scabby cripple had brought the Heartless King nearly to his knees.

*Was this really happening?* Grunt Keefer asked himself. *Would Lucien really fall?*

The guards shifted among themselves, unconsciously drifting toward members of their squads in search of an anchor in the storm.

Yet Lucien had somehow managed to turn the tide. The guards scratched their shoulders, rubbed their necks awkwardly, and peered around hoping no one else had read the doubtful thoughts that had flickered over their faces a moment before.

As Lucien began preparations for the "spectacle to end all spectacles," as he had dubbed it, the guards were relieved to be able to fall into familiar rhythms of behavior. Using spear tips and bludgeon sticks, the crowd was herded around the stage following in the wake of the Heartless King.

The latecomers arriving from sections N7, N9, and S13 were led in by an uncertain-looking group of overseers from the outer guard squadrons. The prisoners shuffled along, looking curious at the unexpected break in routine. But the sour scent of fear soon wafted through the crowd once more as Lucien's preparations neared completion.

Arnion and Lucien were standing in the center of the stage. Someone had handcuffed the ambassador's hands together with a set of rusty iron manacles. They were attached to the top of an all-too-familiar wooden whipping post.

Acadia shuddered at the stories that gouged post could tell. People's skin torn to ribbons. Bloodcurdling screams that no longer sounded human. She had struggled against Eril's grip, but then Has materialized on her other side as well. Somehow, together they had managed to keep her from rushing the stage, but just barely.

As the final work sectors settled into place, the Heartless King stepped forward, leaving Arnion chained in his wake.

"My darling pets, I hope you will forgive this interruption of our daily routine."

His voice nauseated Acadia with its syrupy sweetness.

"But I have a very special announcement. The ambassador from Eiren has been found."

Murmurs swept through the crowd. Lucien allowed them to mumble among themselves for a moment, unsure.

*I'll let their discomfort grow bit by bit,* he relished to himself.

Then, he held up a hand and was met by silence. Lucien couldn't resist a smug grin. They still feared him. No one was going to change that, certainly not after what he was going to do with this ambassador.

"I must say I am a little disappointed that he managed to hide this long right in our very midst," Lucien chided his audience. "And yet he's managed to find his own way here, all by himself."

The Heartless King turned and extended a condescending flourish to the man chained behind him. "Do you know what he's done, my pets?" Lucien paused for dramatic effect, letting his question hang in the air for a moment. "He's offered to pay off all of your debts, all by his little self." Laughing, he turned to face Arnion, pinching his cheek with mock affection.

"I shouldn't have allowed it, but such is the generous nature of your king that I will let him try. Blood for blood," Lucien roared.

The crowd stared back at him in stunned silence.

"Well, what's the matter?" Lucien goaded. "Don't you think he can do it? Where are the cheers for your champion?"

Sneering at Arnion, Lucien tore the ambassador's shirt so that it hung from his waist in tattered folds. Not that it would have done him any good for protection, but the Heartless King wanted everyone to see the damage that was about to be inflicted.

A low keening wail wound its way up from inside Acadia's throat. She could feel her knees shaking. Hers was not the only grief manifesting in the crowd. Eril heard quiet sobs a few rows behind him and turned briefly to meet Agatha's tear-stained face.

Lucien scowled as sounds of mourning drifted up to him on the stage. People didn't grieve for one another in Gehenna. It was one of the first desensitizing traits that was established here. Already annoyed by the weight of the contract burning into his hand, having the crowd sympathize with this worthless ambassador set his teeth on edge. He gestured impatiently to his two heavyweights, Sileen and Purth, to come out from the shadows where they had been lurking.

The guards made their way up the stage with lumbering steps, bludgeon sticks already swinging in anticipation. They both exuded pleasure in their work. Sileen rolled his left shoulder in a stretch, while Purth spit a glob of mucus into the crowd. He grinned at the sounds of disgust as it landed on some unlucky resident. Lucien waved them onward with a flourish.

Making his voice reverberate with the amplification of his spirit, he declared, "And now without further ado, I present to you the spectacle to end all spectacles!"

With a snap of his cape, he drifted to the side and let his beaters begin. It wouldn't do to get splattered. Sileen and Purth were good at their job. The only prerequisite needed was the ability to hurt people, very badly and without compunction. They had a routine when Lucien called them forth. Sileen would go left and Purth to the right. The heavyweights were towering and muscular, each over twenty hands tall, but Sileen had a blunt blocklike head, while Purth's looked more like a whisper weed, accented by a tuft of dirty blond hair sprouting from the crown of his head.

They went to work first on the ambassador's back, inflicting large painful welts with the long, rounded sides of their sticks. This was just a warm-up to see how their victim was going to handle the pain. Would he beg and plead after the first blow? Some soiled themselves at the mere sound of the heavyweights ascending the stage stairs. Others passed out after a few hits. Those were the inconvenient ones because Lucien didn't allow his victims to sleep through anything. Purth would have to keep throwing water in their faces every couple of minutes to keep them conscious.

Sileen thought he might be a fainter from the frail look of him, but the ambassador proved him wrong. He bore the beating with grunts and small gasps of pain, nothing overly theatrical. Lucien would not be pleased if they didn't give him more. Purth nodded at Sileen, and they moved to beating lower along his sides where the ribs were weaker. The Eirenian cried out now, especially after Purth struck a vicious side blow, snaking underneath his ribs to nail his liver.

Arnion gasped and fell to his knees, vision blurring. That last hit had driven all the air out of his lungs. He felt like he couldn't inhale oxygen correctly anymore. The blows continued to rain down on him mercilessly. Painful throbbing enveloped his body. As he fell to his knees, his hands were held upward over his head, still bound to the wooden post. Blows rained down on his arms, his hands, and his back. The jarring rattled the teeth in his skull, and he spit blood after taking a glancing blow to his left cheek. It had split open his lip. He tried to stand, but his left kneecap and the back of his right leg were struck simultaneously, and he clattered back to the ground with a thump.

Arnion's ears were ringing. He could feel the blood pounding through his veins, but the rest of his hearing was a blur. Lucien spoke something, but he couldn't discern what it was. However, it seemed to make the guards pull back in response. Arnion forced himself to his feet with a groan. Focusing on anything took effort, but then there in the crowd, he spotted Acadia's pale face. She was crying. He wanted to smile and tell her that it would be all right, but his face wasn't working properly. It was already starting to swell up. Arnion tried to reach out to her, momentarily forgetting that he was shackled in place. The pressure of the chain against his hands seared him with pain. He felt nausea rise within him like a wave and thought for a moment he might faint. Dizzily, he swayed against the post.

Although it gave Lucien great satisfaction to see the quality beating his heavyweights were giving the ambassador, it wasn't enough. His citizens were still sympathizing with the Eirenian, and it fed Lucien's fury. He was determined to make such a mess of this foolish youth that no one would feel anything but a surge of horror when looking at him.

*I will give them such a show. It will haunt them forever,* he gloated internally.

On top of that, he could still feel the weight of the contract burrowing into his skin. He called the guards to a halt and let the wobbling youth regain his footing before calling out in a harsh voice, "The scourges!"

A murmur of despair burbled through the crowd. Lucien smiled as he noticed those near the front of the stage trying to push farther away from it. His people knew what this meant. Two guards hurried up the stairs to their king carrying bundles swathed in black velvet. Lucien always liked to throw in a touch of elegance where he could, and the black was so much better at hiding the stains.

He had the guards stand facing the crowd and gleefully untied the straps so that the velvet wrappings fell open with a soft swoosh. The scourges glittered in the sunlight. Lucien stroked one wooden handle lovingly. He had taken the basic premise of the whip and perfected it over time to create the most marvelous instrument of pain and public torture imaginable. Attached to each wooden handle were three leather cords made of sagrin hide. Carefully knotted along the hide at regular intervals were broken bits of metal, bone, and glass. Lucien fingered the serrated hook at the end of one of the cords, smiling. It had been inspired by battle he had watched between a scorpion and a desert spider. The Heartless King had decided on a serrated edge for its ability to bite and saw the flesh into ragged slices.

*Let's see how you stand with your foolish compassion now, Ambassador,* he silently mocked.

Lucien raised both arms, and Sileen and Purth trundled forward. They each grabbed hold of a scourge handle and shook it menacingly in front of the crowd. The cords jangled as bits of metal and bone chinked together. Rust-colored flakes of dried blood drifted down to the stage floor. Acadia tightened her grip on Eril's arm painfully, but he did not shake her off. The young man wanted to look away from his friend's pain, but he was transfixed by what was happening. From his peripheral vision, Eril gathered that much of the crowd felt the same way. Arnion was trying to purchase their freedom, but they all knew Lucien would try every underhanded trick in the book to stop him.

*Could Arnion really do it?*

Eril wanted to believe, but the sight of Lucien's horrific weapons made his entrails feel like jelly. The Heartless King called out to the crowd, addressing Arnion without even sparing him a glance.

"What's the matter? You said blood for blood." He minced over to the Eirenian, taunting, "Are you all out of grand declarations so soon, Ambassador?"

The last word was spat out like poisonous venom. Arnion met his gaze, silent but fearless. Beaten and bleeding, he stood firmly before his tormentor and managed to look more regal than the Heartless King in all his glory. Lucien laughed to hide his growing fury. Turning to Sileen, he whispered under his breath, "Finish him!" The guard bobbed his head in a casual bow, eyes hard. Nodding at Purth, they turned back to the prisoner.

The scourges sang out in the air, leather thongs crackling. As the bone and metal bit into his flesh, Arnion could no longer contain his cries of pain. It only took a second for him to realize that the worse agony came when the scourge was pulled back out again, tearing off bloody chunks of his skin. He fell forward on the whipping post, fingers digging into the wood.

The heavyweights continued their assault as the Eirenian's body became a disordered mess of torn flesh. Blood glistened all over him in a sticky sheen and had splattered across the stage. After one particularly fierce lash, the metal claws in Purth's scourge bit so deep that he had trouble pulling it back out again. The guard viciously tugged at it three times before it came free. The ambassador let out a scream of pain that was barely human as a fist-sized wedge of flesh was pulled from his side.

They struck at his chest, his head, and his legs. When the ambassador's quivering form could no longer support his body weight, he fell to his knees and eventually was suspended just above the ground by his arms, still chained to the post. Sileen and Purth continued to whip him, even striking mercilessly at his hands clutching the post until his flensed body was barely recognizable.

Arnion's voice had grown hoarse from screaming. The agony now pinched his lungs closed, and the shallow, rattling breaths he was able to take only wracked his body with spasms. Wheezing, he tried to refocus his blurry vision, but blood kept dripping into his eyes. He could no longer blink. His eyes were swollen from the beatings.

Finally, one of the scourges clattered to the floor. Purth had both hands on his knees, panting. Sileen was also breathing heavily and paused to wipe his profusely sweating brow.

"What's wrong?" Lucien demanded. "Why have you stopped?"

Purth looked up from his panting and rasped, "How is he still alive? I've never seen a man survive a beating like this." The heavy weight hacked and spit a wad of phlegm on the stage. Sileen looked back and forth between the two and nervously shifted the weight between his feet. His arm felt like it was filled with rocks, and his back was sore.

*I should have stretched more*, he mentally chastised himself. True, they hadn't been called upon for a beating like this in a while, so they were a little out of practice. But this Eirenian, it was unnatural how much he could endure. Sileen had never seen anything like it.

Their hesitation was the final straw that snapped Lucien's already fragile self-control.

"I SAID FINISH HIM!" the Heartless King screamed, flecks of spittle flying from his mouth.

His ferocious display had the opposite of its intended effect. The guards stared at him with wide eyes, rooted to the spot in fear.

Malice filled the Heartless King's spirit, unconsciously spilling out onto those around him. He strode forward in a frightful rage and struck Purth in the jaw with a powerful backhanded blow that send him sprawling. Snarling, he grabbed a fistful of Sileen's tunic intending to inflict even worse damage when something just beyond the guard caught his attention. Lucien tossed the guard aside like a piece of rotting fruit.

"Fine then, I'll do it myself!" he roared.

Storming toward a trio of guards standing at the foot of the stage, Lucien snatched a spear from the closest one. He sprinted toward the prisoner, nearly stumbling in his haste, and plunged the spear straight through his chest.

Arnion barely had the strength to open his mouth in a voiceless scream of agony. Pain flooded through his nervous system. He could feel his body shutting down, and then a tremulous voice reached him.

<Arnion?>

It was Acadia's spirit. With the last of his strength, he forced himself to focus and sent her a syna. It was a beautiful grassy field. The wind rippled through in green waves. Clumps of stocky purple flowers were nestled throughout, their silky petals drifting on the wind.

<It's finished, chimad.>

Arnion took his last breath, and Acadia could feel his spirit dissipating as if it was being carried away on the wind.

"No!" She let out an agonized scream and fell to her knees, weeping uncontrollably.

Lucien had also felt the ambassador's death. Staring now at the lifeless corpse before him, he was filled with even more hatred and loathing than before. He kicked at it viscously a few times. Then, taking a ragged breath to regain his composure, he ran his hands through his hair, damp with sweat. Snapping his fingers at the nearest guards, they rushed to do his bidding.

"Get this trash out of my sight," he hissed in contempt.

# CHAPTER 25

Silence filled visio port E-6 with a tangible presence. It was as if their breath had been stolen away, torn from their lungs as they watched the monstrous display unfold before them. Naileah's hands shook. The walls of the visio port had turned transparent and magnified the scene playing on all the grid screens in the room, enhancing it with nanocrystal radiance. The detail and clarity were such that they could have been standing among the crowd rather than watching this tragedy play out from over four hundred stadia away.

*His own father just watched this happen.*

Her mouth went dry, and her head turned involuntarily toward the king. Tears were running down Elyon's face. He made no move to check them. Slowly, he walked toward the visio port wall and reached a hand toward the image of his fallen son's head.

"Lead Analyst!" It was Argo at grid screen 3. "I cannot detect any change in Lucien's contract. The blood oath does not appear to have taken effect."

Naileah's head snapped back toward her staff. "What?" she asked wearily. "Check again. You must be mistaken."

All of the grid screen staff typed furiously, analyzing the footage with irradiated spectrum lenses, frantically scanning for a change in spirit activity.

"Negative."

"Negative."

"Negative."

It was grid screens 2, 3, and 4.

Keturah at grid screen 1 spoke haltingly, "It appears as though the oath is dissolving through the death insurmountable escape clause."

Her grid screen had zeroed in on the image of Lucien's hand bound with the contract. The threads were turning black and fraying. Soon they would fall apart, and he would be released from the oath.

Naileah shook her head. "No, that's not possible." She slammed her hands down on the observation counter, making her staff flinch. "Check again!" She struggled to keep the panic from her tone.

*The prince could not have died for nothing*, she pleaded to herself in despair.

"Grid screen 1, no change reported."

"Grid screen 2, no change reported."

"Grid screen 3, no change reported.

"Grid screen 4, requesting additional confirmation." It was Hazeel, the youngest screen analyst, just barely past her time as an intern. "I think I see something."

Naileah tore over to grid screen 4 and leaned over Hazeel's shoulder. "Show me."

Hazeel pointed a trembling finger at the screen. "It was here just a moment ago." The grid screen was maxed out, focused on the lines of contract fraying around Lucien's wrist. "Here, just for a moment. I thought I saw gold."

Naileah leaned closer and watched the screen intently. The contract lines wrapping around Lucien's right hand and forearm had turned totally black. He was looking down at it and howling with laughter.

*So he knew.* Naileah sighed and closed her eyes, pinching the bridge of her nose between her thumb and index finger.

"There! I saw it again," Hazeel said eagerly.

Naileah opened her eyes and looked down at the grid screen once more. The contract strands were still pure black and ripping apart. Lucien made an obscene gesture.

*Of course, he knew we'd be watching.*

"It's all right, Hazeel." Naileah clapped a hand on the younger girl's shoulder. "This has been a terrible ordeal. I know we all wanted it to turn out differently—"

"Wait!" It was Argo this time, his voice threaded with excitement. "I think I just saw it too!"

All the grid screen staff leaned in closer to their screens, holding their breath. The irradiated spectrum lenses zoomed in on different parts of Lucien's arm, scanning over the cords of the contract. Then Naileah saw it—a flicker of gold twisted along the strand curling up the inside of Lucien's arm. It faded back to black again. She took a deep breath, hands gripping the back of Hazeel's chair like a life support. There it was again—another flash of gold. It was as if the contract was fighting against itself to be fulfilled.

Lucien noticed that something strange was going on as well. He had stopped laughing and was now scowling down at his arm with a fierce intensity. Golden light was pulsing through the black strands now, pushing back the darkness. Lucien gripped his right forearm with his left hand. For a moment, the golden light was pushed back, but then it flooded forward once more, insistent. The Heartless King let go of his arm as if he had been scorched.

The contract burned with a blinding golden light. Its cords twisted around Lucien like an iridescent serpent before rising into the air. Arching over the stage, the luminescent strands split into thousands of tiny threads and went streaking over the audience. For a moment, all the people in Gehenna appeared drenched in heavy chains. The weight of their red contract cords was visibly biting into them, holding them down. The next moment, golden strands chased around each chain, flooding it with light until it burst apart. The smoking remains of contract threads dissolved before they could hit the ground.

"How could this happen?" Lucien bellowed. "They weren't even bound to me. It shouldn't have worked." He fell to his knees as the weight of the spirit transaction sapped him of energy. Lucien pounded the stage weakly with his fists.

*I miscalculated, but how? What did I miss?* His hands clenched, nails digging into the wooden planks.

In Gehenna's compound, people were laughing and crying all at once. The giddy feeling of being released from spiritual bondage flooded through them even if they didn't fully realize why.

Their noise did not reach the Heartless King. He had recessed deep within himself, replaying the scene over and over.

*How could his death have been sufficient? No ordinary ambassador would ever have the authority to break those contracts. They weren't even bound to me. Only someone from the royal line could—*

Lucien's eyes narrowed in understanding. He spit on the stage, picturing the Eirenian king's face.

*Elyon, you are more fanatical than I gave you credit for.*

Lucien stood and brushed the dust from his knees. He knew the Capital City visio ports would be watching his every move, safe in their sparkling towers. Smirking at them with a facetious wave, he clearly mouthed, "This isn't over."

Rubbing his hands together, the Heartless King raced to find a way to use the situation to his advantage. He still had the trividium. Eiren may have delayed his plans, but they would still proceed.

*Just an extended timeline, that's all. But how to twist these freed minds back to me?* he wondered. *Ah, I know.*

"Well, my dearest ones, wasn't that a charming show? Who would have believed the ambassador would truly keep his word?" Lucien put a hand over his heart and wiped away a fake tear. "You are free, my pets. The Prince of Eiren has bought your freedom."

The gasps in the crowd drew a smirk across Lucien's face. It was just as he had suspected. The ambassador had not revealed his identity to the people.

*Now, I will exploit the hole your foolish humility has opened, Little Prince.*

"What's that? You didn't know he was a prince, next in line for the throne? He was that foolish king's sole heir." Lucien jabbed his finger at the crowd. "Do you really want to serve a king like that? Do you really want to pour out your life on behalf of others?" Lucien laughed, a horrible condescending laugh. "If you want to go, then go. I won't stop you. Not even I can cure stupidity."

His voice was scathing, but just as quickly, it smoothed to a soothing purr. "But consider this, my pets. All our hard work has not been in vain. We have discovered something of great power in the mines. Power that I want to share with all of you. Something the Eirenians and that bleeding-heart king of theirs would never allow."

"He wants to keep you from that power, but I want to share it with all of you." Lucien's arm was like a spear as he thrust it toward Eiren.

He paced back and forth along the front of the stage, working himself into a passion. "So what say you? Will you follow that trash to the rubbish heap?" He gestured to the guards who had dragged Arnion's corpse out, leaving a smeared trail of blood along the ground.

"Or will you join me no longer as workers but equals, comrades in arms to take back what's rightfully ours?" The Heartless King extended his hand toward the audience, a beatific smile painting his face.

Acadia rose, shaking. Her breath still came in little hiccups after crying so hard. She swiped at her tears fiercely with the backside of her hand, leaving a streak of dirt along her cheek. Without a word, she turned and followed the bloodstained path around the stage and out the back of the compound. Lucien's mouth was a grim line as others silently followed. He was powerless to stop them—the abhorrent prince's oath had seen to that. But others hesitated. Some looked at him with questioning, fearful eyes. So Lucien pasted on his most cheerful grin. He made his eyes sparkle and his voice light.

"Come, my friends," he said and opened his arms wide to the crowd.

# CHAPTER 26

Burning piles of rubbish smoldered around her as Acadia followed the trail of Arnion's blood. It was here in this small valley that Gehenna originally began as a dumping ground for the nearby city of Beulah's refuse. Rattling carts pulled by broken down sagrins used to dump piles of the city's unmentionables conveniently out of view.

Little by little, groups of people made their way down to the valley, picking over what others had thrown away. Fires were built, shacks cobbled together to break up the wind that howled through during the night. Some were opportunists, looking for a quick way to turn a coin, but most were those the world had cast out. Untouchables they were called. Curse or sickness drove them from the dwellings of others.

People wondered why Lucien was so eager to take possession of this burning dung heap. It was one of Elorah's greatest mysteries until the trividium veins hidden deep underground were unearthed. Rumors used to flicker through every few years that he feasted on the misery that had soaked into the land for so many years.

Acadia was too consumed by grief to appreciate a deep analysis of the symbolism interwoven in Gehenna's past history at the moment. She felt as if she was made of stone, each step slow and heavy. Plodding through the gravel, she shuffled her feet as if they weighed too much to actually lift off the ground.

All the colors and sounds seemed muted. It was as if Arnion took all the brightness and clarity out of the world with his spirit when he left. She tried to make herself focus to think about what she should do now, but everything was a blank. Her mind was a white haze of pain. All she knew was that she wanted to be near Arnion, so she forced herself to walk, smudging the trail his body had left along the ground.

She was not aware of the others who followed her, Eril, Has, and Agatha, of course. But there were more, many more than Acadia would have ever dreamed possible if her mind hadn't clamped down into a self-protective mode that was barely conscious. Even a few of the guards laid down their arms and followed her out.

Gehenna lost more than half of her workforce that day. Many who had gathered with Arnion to share water had followed her. Many but not all. Then there were others from the distant work sections, the farthest reaches of Sector N and Sector S, who had not heard Arnion's message directly but were moved by his bravery or disgusted with Lucien's cruelty. As the chains of their contracts broke, minds cleared. The stranglehold of despair and hopelessness was broken. They were not compelled to stay in Gehenna any longer, so they followed Acadia. Like a defeated army, they crept along, heads bowed, silent.

She thought she had no more tears left to cry. It felt like she had cried an ocean from inside of her. But when she saw his broken body, lying there amid the crumpled paper, broken glass, and stained rags, Acadia fell to her knees. She touched a shaking hand to her cheek and felt the tears coursing down.

*I never want to feel anything ever again.*

It was as if she was one of those discarded scraps of cloth, and someone had torn her into the jagged pieces littering the ground.

*Is this what my life will be from now on?*

She heard a wretched, wailing sound, and it took her a long time before she realized the sound was coming from her own throat. Acadia pressed her forehead into the ground, blind to the pain as little bits of debris cut into her skin.

Soft bells tinkled in the distance. Feet clad in delicate shoal skin, and silk whispered across the sand, anklets jingling with the mourning bells of Eiren. King Elyon had arrived with his retinue.

The passenger conveyors had landed behind the lip of a sand dune, obscuring their approach. As the occupants crested the hill, some of the Gehennians who had followed Arnion drew back in alarm. Dressed all in white, the Eirenians seemed to glide over the ground like phantasms. Standard-bearers bore a muted version of the royal crest woven in pale gray thread over white tsochi cloth. They fluttered in the wind without making a sound. Eirenian mourning customs dictated that no noise should be made throughout the proceedings other than the funerary charms worn on each participants' ankles.

This made it all the more shocking when King Elyon bent down before Acadia and extended his hand toward her.

"Come, my child."

Those in the funeral retinue were too well seasoned to betray any outward signs of surprise they may have felt. Their king had always been compassionate. Even the death of his only son on behalf of these people wouldn't change that.

Somehow, the king's voice reached her, like throwing a rope to a drowning man. Acadia lifted her head and met the kind expression in his gaze.

*So familiar…*

Her mind wanted to shrink away from the surge of pain that this realization brought with it, but her heart won out, and she took hold of the hand that was offered. The king helped her to her feet.

By this time, the bereavement transport had also landed. Its crew, with a glimmering white stretcher that hovered in midair, lined up quietly behind their ruler. Elyon gave them a slight nod, and the team gently lifted Arnion onto the stretcher. Acadia stared at the broken fingers peeking over the edge.

The sight of his shattered child was nearly unbearable to Elyon. He reached out and rested a hand on his child's head, matted with blood.

"My son," he whispered.

The pain in his voice drew Acadia's gaze.

*Arnion's…father…?* she realized, dazed.

She turned to face him and took in the man before her for the first time, not the fact that he was a king. That thought was still beyond her grief-addled mental capacity for the moment. Acadia looked at him and saw a man, strong and broad shouldered, who had become hunched over in unbearable sorrow. His grief rolled off of him in waves, so thick it was tangible. She didn't know any words she could say or anything she could do to make this situation right. All she could think of was to reach out and embrace him, pressing their sorrow into a hot white ball that burned between them.

Appalled at the disregard shown for their king's station, Genoas stepped forward intent on separating them. Maulki put a calm hand on his forearm and shook his head. Genoas knew he couldn't voice his disapproval vocally, but as he saw King Elyon return the embrace and kiss the top of the girl's head, his annoyance evaporated. If his king could accept this unconventional, albeit heartfelt expression of condolence, who was he to argue? Shoulders sagging, Genoas turned to survey the crowd.

The Lead Analyst's advice had been spot on. As Naileah monitored the conclusion of the blood contracts, she predicted that they would need many more personnel transports to bring back all the newly freed Gehennians, and she was right. Lucien had not been able to maintain hold over many of his subjects at all. Thankfully, her advice was followed to the letter. Genoas could see the additional transports preparing to land. Soon, they would have to break the silence in order to provide instructions to the Gehennians, dividing them into groups for transport. The hover ships would carry them all to Eiren where King Elyon would welcome them into his kingdom, just as he had always wanted. However, Genoas hoped the bereavement and accompanying mourning retinue would be able to leave first. He looked uncertainly at his king.

After kissing the top of Acadia's head, Elyon took the young woman's hand in his. "Come."

He gestured toward the transports. Acadia followed his gesture till her eyes landed on the passenger conveyor. She was too numb to be surprised. However, when the bereavement team began to move the stretcher toward a different transport, she jerked her hand out of his grasp, shaking her head.

Some of the mourners stepped forward with chastising looks, but Elyon waved them away.

"Let her be. She may ride with my son and me."

Those in his retinue fell back instantly, and Acadia was allowed to follow the stretcher bearing Arnion's body to the bereavement transport. After they had lifted him in, she climbed in beside him, sitting on one of the benches that lined either side of the vehicle. While the seat looked hard, it was comfortable. She reached out and took hold of Arnion's hand, running a thumb over his knuckles.

As the transport hummed to life, weblike bands of yellow light snapped across her waist and shoulders like a harness, securing her in place. She looked up in alarm, but upon meeting the calm gazes of the other passengers, Acadia realized this must be normal for an Eirenian transport. Her fears soothed, Acadia returned her attention to rubbing her thumb against the back of Arnion's hand and tried not to think.

The Eirenians laid their prince to rest in a tomb, but it was more like a glittering crystal vault in Acadia's opinion. The sunlight shone through, enhanced by refractor prisms into a dazzling array of colors. Twelve freshly planted saplings circled the round room, and the carpet was a plush green moss, springy underfoot. In the center was a quietly murmuring stream, which she was told fed the moss and trees through tiny irrigation capillaries that ran underneath the floor. Over time, the trees would grow thicker, and little white flowers, shaped like stars, would dot the mossy floors. Rising in the center of the stream was a stone pillar so brilliantly white that it almost hurt the eye to look at it. There in an ornately carved stone coffin, they laid him.

Acadia was still having trouble feeling anything. World-shattering revelations, like the fact that Arnion was a prince or that she had hugged the King of Eiren, barely registered with her at all. In a nation consumed by grief, her faux pas went generally unnoticed. At the most, they were met with mild smiles of tolerance.

Rhys, who she learned was Arnion's close advisor and friend, seemed to have taken a deeply rooted interest in her well-being. He kept encouraging her to do things like eat and speak, which felt impossible.

Lying awake on her electrostasis net for hours, Acadia would stare at the tufted ceiling before drifting into a restless sleep. The Eirenian bed emitted soothing wavelike sounds that were supposed to help her doze off, but every time she closed her eyes, she could still picture Arnion's wordless scream as Lucien ran him through. Rhys assured her that electrostasis nets were the latest Eirenian technology to help with recovering physical and emotional well-being, but Acadia still wasn't sold on it.

*Call me old-fashioned, but sleeping on a hovering electric field above a spallo gel pod is a little unnerving.*

It did perfectly contour to her body and had autonomous heat regulators that circulated air around her at the perfect temperature to enjoy a restful night's sleep.

*But half the time, I thrash around so much in my sleep that I wake myself up.*

The electrostasis net would deactivate when the nightmares became too violent. More than once, Acadia found herself wallowing around on the spallo gel mattress, disoriented and confused. Her thermal foil blankets wrapped around her limbs like manacles. Whenever the first shaft of the dawn sun pierced her window, she would power down the bed and stumble toward the tomb once more. Acadia would sit on a clump of moss close to the stream, its dampness soaking into her new skirts, and she would listen to the babbling water.

The first day, she had waded into the stream and pressed her cheek against the cold stone box. When Rhys found her and had to cross through the water himself to pry her away that night, he looked so pitiful in his sopping wet robes that Acadia silently resolved not to make him do it again. He never complained or spoke an unkind word, but he was grieving too, she could tell.

*The last think I want to do is make anyone around here more miserable than they already are,* she thought to herself. *Everyone has been so kind.*

Acadia laid her head down onto the mossy floor, suddenly tired. The murmurs of the stream lulled her into sweet sleep.

# CHAPTER 27

The world was bleached of color. Dark clouds churned overhead. Arnion awoke to find himself on a narrow path, hewn between large rocky outcroppings. Gasping, he felt around his chest with both hands where the spear had pierced him. Nothing was there.

*Where is it?*

Just a moment ago, he had felt the metal point rip through his chest like a consuming fire, feeding on his very life. Now, he felt—nothing.

He had an even greater shock when he looked down at his hands and then the rest of his body. It was as if all the color and substance had been sucked out of him to match his surroundings. He was still wearing the torn shirt and pants from moments before, but they were no longer soaked with his blood. His olive skin had turned a pale gray like the belly of a dead fish. When he looked closely, his entire being was slightly translucent and giving off a faint glow.

*Where am I?* he wondered.

The sound of rushing wind filled the air, and yet Arnion could feel no breeze. Not a speck of dust stirred. He did a quick scan of his surroundings. But there was nothing. Not a single living thing. Just rock formations as far as the eye could see.

*And this path.*

Arnion bent down and ran a hand over it. Small, beaded pebbles lined the way, each exactly the same shape and size. He plucked one up and examined it between his fingertips. The stone was slightly iridescent, like a gray pearl, rounded on one side and completely flat on the other. Lining the path in miniscule rows, they continued off into the distance.

*Interesting, but it doesn't help me get out of here.*

Sighing, he replaced the pebble in the tiny gap he had created. It snicked back into place as if pulled by magnetic force.

"Hello?" Arnion shouted into the vastness before him. The air seemed to swallow up his words. Nothing stirred. He felt completely alone.

*So this is death.*

There was no denying it any longer. He had felt himself die.

*I wonder what Acadia's doing now.*

A blade of sadness pierced his heart, and he winced, clutching a hand to his chest. Taking a deep breath, he shook his head and surveyed his surroundings once more.

Off in the distance to his left, Arnion thought he saw a flash of color out of the corner of his eye.

*What was that?*

It reminded him of his father's robes, a deep amethyst inlaid with spun golden thread.

*But why would Father be here? I must be hallucinating.*

He took a step off the path, intending to investigate. The air shrieked overhead, and green bolts of lightning crackled in the sky. Shadows seemed to twine around the rocks, writhing in agitation. Surprised, Arnion took a step backward. Once he was back on the trail, the surroundings returned to their normal state.

*At least normal for this place*, he mused.

He walked forward a few paces over the small stones, and nothing extraordinary happened. "I'm supposed to stay on the path, is that it?" he asked the emptiness around him.

A heavy silence pressed down on him in response.

"Tsk," he clucked his tongue unconsciously, thinking. *What am I supposed to do now? Walk along this lonely path for an eternity?*

There again, to his left, a flicker of purple teased the corner of his peripheral vision. Whipping around to track the movement, Arnion swore he saw his father disappearing behind a cluster of boulders.

*It looked just like his silhouette, but why? How could my father be here?*

Testing the environment's reaction, he pressed his toes up to the very edge of the beaded path. Nothing happened. Arnion flexed his feet and was surprised when he couldn't crack his big toes like he usually did.

*I guess there's no knuckle cracking in the afterlife.* He smiled wistfully to himself.

An image of Elyon again flitted between the boulders. The figure paused, looking back over his shoulder to meet Arnion's puzzled stare. The prince was rooted to the spot in bewilderment. It was too far to make out the details of the king's expression, but his son could spot that craggy outline anywhere.

"Father!" he cried out, voice breaking.

The shadowy visage turned away without reply but gestured with his hand for the prince to follow.

Arnion did not hesitate. He took off like a shot toward his father's image. As he expected, the shadows seemed to shriek angrily at him the moment he stepped off the marked path. The further he went from it, the more frenzied everything became.

His glimpses of Elyon grew more frequent, flitting just ahead of him around corners or ducking around a twisted clump of stone. Arnion was gaining on him, but the landscape also seemed to be physically fighting his approach. The air felt like it was congealing around him. Arnion was forced to slow his run as he pushed forward. It felt like he was wading through a gelatinous ooze. The sensation was horrendously disconcerting, and yet he knew that he had to reach his father no matter what.

He could see Elyon slip behind a clawlike rock formation.

*Like the talons of a grimlock.*

Arnion felt exhausted. He wanted to stop, but he knew that his father was waiting just beyond his sight for him to follow.

*I just have to get beyond this last outcropping.*

The prince rallied his strength.

*I must find out why he's here.*

A sense of dread suddenly filled him, and Arnion hesitated. In his gut or whatever passed for a gut in this shadow realm, he sensed a malevolent intent gathering around him. He shifted his feet into a fighting stance, angling his body to the side to reduce the area that an enemy could target. Raising his arms up to protect his head, he chose an open-hand position for its versatility. Arnion pressed his fingertips together, imagining the Eirenian self-defense practicums he had memorized early in his youth, and waited.

He did not have long to wait. Snapping and coiling, the shadows contorted into jagged angles. Refracting against each other, the angular shapes broke apart into grotesque limbs and claws. Creatures out of the blackest nightmares stitched themselves together before him, forming a wall between Arnion and the rocky fingers where his father had stopped. The shadows clustered together so thickly that the way was completely obscured from view. Monstrous jaws snapped at him and tentacles thrashed, driving him back toward the path.

"No!" Arnion shouted. "I'm not going back there."

This seemed to infuriate the shadow wraiths further. Where their limbs touched him, he was seized by an intense cold that would have frozen the blood in his veins if he still had any. Arnion tried to pry their talons off of him as they converged around him, but it was no use. His actions just seemed to drive the maniacal beasts further into a frenzy. Darkness swallowed him in its icy maw.

He tried to beat against the obsidian wall with his fists, but they bounced off as if striking rubber. The suffocating gloom was pressing in on his eyes, creeping up into his ears, and tightening against his throat. In that moment, he knew the creatures would carry him back to the path and force him to walk down it, alone.

Images of Acadia floated through his mind. He remembered her rough fingers brushing against his to take the cup of water, the way her hand trembled when he led her away from the lecherous guards, and the kiss they shared as the sandstorm raged around them.

Then, Lucien's wicked grin rose in Arnion's mind. The Heartless King rubbed his hands together, triumphant with glee at discovering a fresh source of trividium. Arnion knew that even now, that horrible creature was scheming all the ways to inflict misery and suffering on the world.

"Let it go," the darkness susurrated all around him. "None of it matters anymore. Let it go."

It pressed against him like a velvet cloth, heavy, caressing. He felt its smothering tentacles tighten around him, trying to pry the memories from his mind.

Just when Arnion thought all hope was lost, a light pierced through the darkness. He heard his father's spirit resound in his head.

<In your darkest hour, a light will shine forth and lead you unto victory.>

And Arnion remembered—everything. He closed his eyes, fingers curling into fists at his sides. The darkness around him let on a scream of despair as power coursed through him, a blinding white light that rippled over his body in waves.

Instead of the bitter cold, Arnion now felt an intense warmth burning from within him. He could feel his spirit blazing with power, so strong he could barely contain it. Trying to find an outlet for the tremendous energy flowing through him, Arnion channeled it through his right arm and out his fingertips. He could feel it growing and solidifying around them.

Arnion opened his eyes with a crackle of electricity. The power burning behind them shined a fierce white light. He looked down at his right hand that was now clutching a blade hewn from the force that flowed through him. Flickers of electricity crackled along its surface, and the blade itself seemed composed of incandescent light. It was a two-handed greatsword, at least ten hands in length. Yet it felt nearly weightless in his grip. Arnion examined it, astounded.

*This sword came from my spirit?*

The darkness yowled and spat at him. Arnion lifted the sword above his head and with a strong downward stroke, tore a jagged hole in it from top to bottom. As shards of the creature fell away, a cloying stench, like rotting flowers, filled the air.

"Release me," he commanded, and like a whipped dog, it crouched before him and fled, clambering over the rocks and then out of sight.

Arnion found himself where he had first planted his feet in the fighting stance. The darkness, for all of its manipulations, had not been able to carry him one step.

He flexed his fingers around the hilt and took an experimental swing. It felt as natural as breathing. Arnion smiled.

*A sword of the spirit. Let's see what it can do.*

Swinging it across a boulder on his right, the sword cut through the rock as if it was made of hot butter. Where the blade had passed through, cracks widened in the stone until it shattered apart into a pile of dust. Eyes wide, Arnion bent down to touch the pulverized boulder with his fingertips. There was nothing left of it but a fine powder.

The blade hummed between his hands. He could feel it pulsing with energy from his spirit. Arnion closed his eyes and stretched out his spirit's awareness over the land. It traveled over the realms of the dead and returned to him. He knew it all completely. Eyes still shut, Arnion lifted his sword of the spirit in both hands and tore a hole in the fabric of the world.

# CHAPTER 28

As the first rays of morning sunlight threaded their way in through the vaulted windows of her room, Acadia's eyes popped open. She slithered out from under her tangled mess of sheets and blankets, blinking against the light.

*I've got to get back.*

Her bare feet sank into the rich maroon carpet on the floor. Shuffling over to the wardrobe, she pulled her night shift over her head and left it in a heap on the ground. Absently, she scratched at her knuckles. The smoke rash was starting to heal, but it was an engrained habit.

A memory of Arnion swam into her mind. "Please don't, chi-mad," he whispered, covering her hand with his.

Acadia snatched her hand away with a cry and dug her fingers into the stubble of hair around her temples.

*Arnion, I miss you.* She had lost the sense of time passing since he died. *Days, hours, what does it matter anymore?*

Acadia couldn't bear to think of it, so she pushed it from her mind. Digging through the glossy ruewood wardrobe, she dressed herself mechanically, not caring whether the patterns and colors matched.

*The things I used to care so much about, it seems like a lifetime ago.*

She sighed and rubbed a hand over her prickly scalp, biting her lip.

*I've got to get back to him. I'm already later than usual.*

The Eirenians had given her a beautiful pair of shoal-skin slippers, pale yellow with tiny crystals sewn into the rim in the shape of flowers. Half the time, Acadia forgot to put them on at all and slipped through the palace barefoot. She caught sight of them beside a chair by the door.

*I'd only take them off when I get there anyway.*

She shrugged and left them.

Acadia crept down the passageway to the tomb. She kept her head down. It was unbearable to see the pitying glances of those around her or, worse yet, the raw grief in Eirenian eyes as they tried to force themselves to smile at her.

*I just want to be near him. I can't take anything else right now.*

Tucking her chin down toward her chest, she hurried on.

The doors to the tomb were enormous, carved with elaborate designs of flora and fauna. Acadia couldn't recognize most of it and realized they must be species specific to Eiren. She hadn't taken the time to examine it closely yet, but she couldn't help glancing at a gorgeous butterfly carved right at eye level. Its wings were made of stained glass in stunning shades of purple and green. The sculptor's talent was truly impressive. The creature looked like it was about to leap off of the carving and fly out an open window.

Shaking her head sadly, Acadia activated the pneumatic hinges that made the doors nearly weightless. They swung open at the gentle touch of her hand and closed automatically a few seconds after the sensors indicated she had entered.

Acadia took a few of staggering steps inward and fell to her knees with a heartrending scream. There in the center of the stream was the stone pillar, and upon it, Arnion's pristine coffin looked like it had been sheared in two. It had been struck with such force that pieces had flown across the stream, embedding themselves in the mossy embankment. Splinters of stone prickled the young saplings growing within the tomb.

"No, no, no," Acadia moaned, crawling forward. Tears filled her eyes, and she gathered pieces of the tomb that she could find, trying to fit them back together. "This can't... Why would someone..."

She thought her heart had already fractured beyond repair, but this final desecration of Arnion's remains broke a well of deep sorrow within her greater than she had ever known.

*Why couldn't they just leave him in peace?*

Acadia collapsed on the ground, sobbing.

"Why are you crying?" a male voice asked from behind her.

Acadia didn't have the energy left to be surprised.

"Can't you see?" she asked, voice hoarse. "They've taken him away, and I don't know where they've put him." She started to cry once more, and she felt the stranger crouch down beside her.

"Who is it you're looking for?" he asked her, gently placing a hand on her shoulder.

Acadia shook his arm off and looked up, annoyed.

*Who is this person? Is he mocking me?*

Sniffling, she wiped her nose on her sleeve and gave him the once-over. He was handsome, with beautiful tawny skin. Short, dark curls framed his face, and golden-brown eyes surveyed her with genuine concern.

*I've never seen him around here before*, she thought suspiciously. Then an idea flashed through her mind. *Maybe he's the one who took Arnion!*

Acadia grabbed him by the collar, shaking him fiercely. "If you've carried him away, tell me where he is! Tell me, and I'll go and get him back!"

The young man laughed, eyes twinkling. She was just about to shake him again, harder this time, when she felt a voice in her spirit.

<Acadia, it's me!>

A familiar syna filled her mind of a windswept grassy field and heady purple flowers. It was the exact same image Arnion had sent her right before he died.

*But that's not possible!*

She felt a sound like a roaring wind, and it took a moment to realize it was the feeling of blood rushing to her head. Acadia pressed a hand to her forehead and tried to focus.

*I saw him die.*

Of that, she was certain. Living in Gehenna, she had become personally acquainted with death.

*But that syna and that spirit, it was so familiar.*

Her heart skipped a beat.

"A-Arnion?" she stuttered, grip relaxing in shock. "Is it really you?"

"Yes!" he replied with his voice this time, bringing his hands up to cup her face.

Her bottom lip trembled, and tears threatened to blur her vision. "But how? Why? You don't—" She broke off and swiped at her eyes with the corner of her sleeve. She looked him over once more, blushing. "You don't *look* like you."

Arnion drew her to him in a tight embrace. "It's me, Acadia." He ran a hand soothingly over her scalp, and she relaxed into him. "My appearance was modified before entering Gehenna. I'm sorry if I frightened you just now."

"Nuh-uh," she mumbled, pressing her face into the space where his neck met his shoulder. He smelled earthy and fresh. Acadia drank in his scent. "I missed you so much," she whispered into his skin.

"I missed you too."

He pressed a kiss against her temple. Acadia crinkled her nose.

*It was impossible. So impossibly good, the best news ever in the history of time! So why do I feel like I'm about to...*

She couldn't stop herself from weeping. Arnion held her close as she sobbed into his shoulder, hot tears staining his shirt.

And that was how the palace staff found them, much to Acadia's mortification later on when she could reflect on it. Her first shriek had alerted the guard. Rhys rushed in, followed by a number of attendants and security staff. Amid their shouts of surprise and delight, Acadia reluctantly released the crown prince to his subjects. The nation was filled with weeping once more but this time of incredible joy rather than sorrow. Their prince had returned from the realm of the dead. It was unheard of, impossible, completely Arnion.

Acadia had never known such feasting and celebration as what took place in the next few weeks. Ballads were sung, and epic poems composed. Palace staff tapped their feet to the catchier verses unconsciously. They knew the battle was not over, but their prince had been returned to them, and they couldn't contain their delight. Acadia had never known someone so loved as Arnion, and she had never known someone so deserving of love.

The Gehennians who had followed him were welcomed into the kingdom of Eiren. Eirenian families volunteered as sponsors, cooking meals and offering classes on the culture and monetary system. Rhys worked tirelessly to see that their needs were met. The first few days were rife with misunderstandings. Some of the Gehennians were half wild from living in Lucien's compounds for so long. Getting them to sleep, eat, and bathe in a way that the Eirenians were accustomed to did not happen overnight. Things progressed more smoothly once Arnion suggested that Eril and Has be appointed as supervisors over the integration process.

*They rose to the occasion magnificently*, Acadia thought, smiling. She had been doing that a lot lately, so much that her face was starting to hurt. *I guess those muscles started to atrophy during my time in Gehenna. Well, they're certainly getting a good workout now.*

All it took was one glimpse of Arnion alive and well to send her over the moon with happiness. Eril called her joy infectious. The Gehennians laughed and cried so much in that first week that Acadia had a sneaking suspicion Rhys had begun slipping calming herbal supplements into everyone's tea.

One day, in the midst of all the boisterous celebrations, Arnion took her hand in his and slipped them away from the crowds. "Come. I want to show you something, chimad." His voice was eager.

Looking up to meet his smiling gaze took her breath away. He led her to a familiar field, one she recognized instantly.

"Arnion, this is just like the syna you sent me."

His grip on her hand tightened. "Yes, it's one of my favorite places in all the world. I wanted to bring you here so badly, but I didn't think it would be possible before." His voice drifted off, quiet.

Acadia examined his contemplative expression wordlessly. She had tried asking him about his experience in the realm of the dead, but his answers were vague, evasive.

"I remembered who I was" was all he would say. Clearly, he wanted more time to process everything on his own. Acadia smothered her innate desire to pry deeper and let it go.

*For now, at least.* She grinned to herself. *I'll get it out of him eventually.*

"Let's lay down and look at the clouds." She tugged at his arm like a little child, and he smiled, breaking out of his reverie. They lay down next to each other, grass tickling their skin, fingers entwined. Puffy white clouds scudded lazily overhead.

Acadia tried to relax, but she kept hearing this strange sound. *What is that?*

Finally, she couldn't take it any longer and sat up, looking around.

"What's wrong?" Arnion propped himself up on an elbow, eyeing her with concern.

"Nothing really." Acadia looked down, embarrassed. "I just keep hearing this strange noise."

"Strange noise?" Arnion looked around. After a few breaths of silently scanning the area, he caught her gaze. "I don't hear or sense anything out of the ordinary."

Acadia could feel herself blushing. "It's this weird, whispery, fluttering sound."

She felt the warm breeze kiss her face and tracked its movement across the grass. "Oh!" she gasped in surprise, finally recognizing what the mysterious sound was.

Arnion followed her gaze to the edge of the field, lined with columns of ruewood trees. Their broad, green leaves shimmered in the wind. "The trees?" he queried, raising an eyebrow.

She clutched his arm, tears shinning in her eyes. "It's the sound of the wind blowing through the leaves. I'd forgotten what that sounds like!"

Laughing, she pressed a soft kiss to the corner of his mouth. Arnion was about to deepen the kiss when a royal insignia flashed through his mind.

<Urgent message for His Highness, the crown prince. We have a diplomatic situation!>

The message finished with directions guiding him and a list of designated guests, to include his father and the royal advisors, to conference room 380B as soon as possible.

Arnion sighed and fingered the matching engagement armbands that he had smuggled out in the pocket of his robes. They were handmade of spun gold, a simple design of braided cords intertwined. Arnion's heart had pounded as he wove the braid himself and formed the two armbands from the same weave. He had carved out two delicate sapphire roses. *For Acadia's radiant eyes,* he had thought when choosing the gemstone and twined each stem around the paws of a golden lion, the symbol of his royal family.

It had been hard to find an opportunity to speak to her alone.

*Not that I begrudge anyone wanting to celebrate. I'll just have to be patient. We have time.*

The thought made him squeeze the armbands tightly for a moment before letting them fall deeper into his pocket. He released a breath he didn't realize he'd been holding. Pulling himself up to his feet, he reached down to help her up.

"Come, chimad. We have work to do."

# AUTHOR'S NOTE

I hope that you enjoyed Arnion and Acadia's adventure. This story is meant to be a picture of our relationship with Jesus Christ, who came down to earth and died on our behalf, but the saga doesn't end there. In the greatest love story of all time, Romeo doesn't stay dead.

Of course, I've taken a lot of liberty with my interpretation, but I hope you'll stop to consider: You are loved more than you could ever possibly imagine. There is a God who created you, and you are incredibly precious to him.

So precious in fact that he sent his son to die for you so that you can live forever with him in heaven.

You see, just like the people trapped in Gehenna, all of us have become trapped in what God calls sin. No matter how much good we do, we'll never earn enough points to buy our way into heaven. The standard is perfection, and let's face it, humans just aren't very great at that. God saw that we weren't going to make it, and so he mounted a rescue mission.

The only one who could ever possibly meet that perfect standard was God himself, and so God came down in the person of Jesus Christ. He died in place of you and me so that we don't have to meet that perfect standard anymore. All we have to do is believe and receive his free gift of eternal life.

If you have doubts, ask God to reveal himself to you. He's big enough to handle your doubts, your questions, even your anger. Jesus made a promise, "Ask and it will be given to you; seek and you will find; knock and the door will be opened to you. For everyone who asks receives; the one who seeks finds; and to the one who knocks, the door will be opened" (Matthew 7:7–8). If you genuinely seek to know God, you will absolutely find him because he loves you and he wants you to know him.

If you'd like to invite God into your life right now, just ask him! It can be as simple as saying something like

> *Dear Jesus,*
> *I want to know you. Please forgive me for the wrong things I've done in my life. Thank you for dying in my place. I believe you were raised to life again and are preparing a place for me to be with you together in eternity. Please show me how much you love me. Help me to believe and love you with everything I have and to love others as you have loved me.*
> *Amen.*[1]

This isn't some magic spell that's suddenly going to make everything in your life perfect. But it does mean that there's someone who loved you enough to die for you, and you can always go to him for help, no matter how dark things get.

If you were impacted by this and want to reach out, you can contact me through <u>pamelahartwrites.com</u>. I would love to meet you!

---

[1] "Amen" comes from the Hebrew language. It's an affirmation roughly translated as "so be it."

# GET CONNECTED!

Keep in touch with Pamela at <u>pamelahartwrites.com</u>.

- Get special access to her latest novella, *City of a Thousand Tears*
- Find out more about Arnion and Acadia's upcoming adventures
- Write to Pamela Hart through the contact page
- Sign up for Pamela's newsletter to get updates on free short stories, deleted scenes, and more

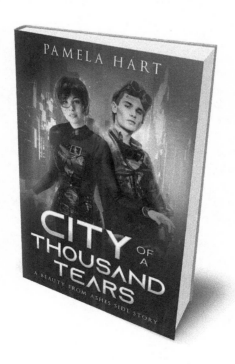

# SHARE YOUR VOICE

Thank you for reading *Beauty from Ashes*.

If you enjoyed this book, would you consider leaving a review on <u>Goodreads</u> or the store you purchased it from?

Whether you loved the story or had suggestions for improvement, honest reviews help readers discover new books and help authors learn more about creating stories you'll love.

# ACKNOWLEDGMENTS

*Beauty from Ashes* was inspired by a creative outreach we did with YWAM Tokyo during our Discipleship Training School in 2012. I would like to thank my dear friends who worked with me on the comic that sparked the flame of writing inside my soul. Thank you, Rebecca Halverson, for co-writing that original comic with me and for helping me learn to follow Jesus with passion. Thank you, Lindsey Leung, for your masterful Japanese translation. Thank you, Hannah Zieber, Daniel Lilly, and Kaare Thiessen, for your awesome illustrations. I also want to thank our leaders, David McDaniel, Greg Lilley, and Rachel Lilley, for being amazing role models, showing us what it looks like to live in lifelong pursuit of Christ.

Thank you to my lovely beta readers, Ashley Wartonick, Diana Chiriboga-Flor, and Carrie Kneeland. Without your enthusiasm, I would have given up on *Beauty from Ashes* long ago. I will always be grateful for the encouragement you gave me.

To Wendy Meyer, my publication specialist, thank you very much for your patience with me dragging out the editing process much longer than it needed to be. Thank you for taking the time to talk with me and go over all my questions as a new author.

To the folks at Christian Faith Publishing, thank you for giving me a chance to share *Beauty from Ashes* with the world.

To the amazing computer wizards at T-Systemo, thank you for rescuing *Beauty from Ashes* after my hard drive crashed. When I thought all hope was lost, you saved the day. Grazie mille, ragazzi! A special shoutout to Enrico for his amazing English language skills and for helping me remain calm during a very stressful point in my writing career.

Willy and Marvin, my beloved packmates, thank you for sitting beside me during hours of writing and editing when what you really wanted to do was play fetch or snuggle.

To my dashing rascal of a husband, thank you for supporting me. Without you, none of this would have been possible. Loving you is a grand adventure, and we're only just getting started.

To the one who loved me first, Jesus Christ, my Lord and Savior, thank you for loving me, rescuing me, and setting me free.

# ABOUT THE AUTHOR

Pamela Hart is the author of *Beauty from Ashes*. Raised on a steady diet of fantasy, science fiction, and anime, she spent most of her childhood failing to acquire a Boston accent. Since then, she has slurped ramen in Ikebukuro, stampeded through flamenco lessons in Granada, and splashed her way across a fishpond for the Milkman Triathlon in Dexter. During her travels, she tends to overpack horrendously but never regrets cramming her backpack full of books to devour along the way. She roams the planet in search of adventure with Joe, the love of her life, and her adorably maniacal Boston terriers, Willy and Marvin.